Praise for *Bridge of Gold*

"Kimberley Woodhouse is a must-read for me! Her grasp on historical fiction is delightful and the stories she weaves leave me eagerly anticipating her next tale!"
— Jaime Jo Wright, Daphne du Maurier and Christy Award–winning author of *The Haunting at Bonaventure Circus*

"What a refreshing, original story! *Bridge of Gold* captured me from start to finish. Author Kimberley Woodhouse deftly navigates both the historical and contemporary timelines, steering me as a reader through rich details and vibrant settings, intrigue, romance, and danger. In the end, I found myself in the safe harbor of timeless faith, courage, and love. Another winning tale from an author I trust!"
— Jocelyn Green, Christy Award–winning author of *Shadows of the White City*

"What better place to lose yourself in love than old San Francisco during the years of building the Golden Gate Bridge. Kimberley Woodhouse has outdone herself with this fabulous duo romance, complete with edge-of-your-seat suspense. Don't miss it!"
— Hannah Alexander, author of *Some Kind of Hero*

"Kimberley Woodhouse is a master at historical romance, and it's nearly impossible to find her equal."

–Colleen Coble, *USA Today* bestselling author of *The View from Rainshadow Bay* and the Rock Harbor series

"Kimberley Woodhouse is one of my very favorite authors, as most of my readers know. Kim has a way with words and plotlines that keeps me turning pages until I've completed the book with a satisfied sigh. I think readers will be very happy with her stories and *Bridge of Gold*, her latest offering, is no exception."

–Tracie Peterson, award-winning, bestselling author of over one hundred novels

BRIDGE

of

GOLD

BRIDGE

of

GOLD

KIMBERLEY WOODHOUSE

BARBOUR
PUBLISHING

Bridge of Gold

©2021 by Kimberley Woodhouse

Print ISBN 978-1-64352-957-8

eBook Editions:
Adobe Digital Edition (.epub) 978-1-64352-959-2
Kindle and MobiPocket Edition (.prc) 978-1-64352-958-5

Photograph: Lee Avison / Trevillion Images

Published by Barbour Publishing, Inc., 1810 Barbour Drive, Uhrichsville, Ohio 44683, www.barbourbooks.com

Our mission is to inspire the world with the life-changing message of the Bible.

Member of the
Evangelical Christian
Publishers Association

Printed in the United States of America.

This book is lovingly dedicated to Kayla and Steven Whitham.
You two are precious to me and Dad. It was absolutely
amazing to see how God brought you together. We thank God
for you each and every day.

You survived and thrived in 2020—through a long-
distance relationship, a global pandemic, natural disasters,
lockdowns, travel restrictions, protests, riots, and all the
other craziness that will be remembered as the year most
people couldn't wait to put behind them. In the midst of
the chaos, we have had a year of celebration and joy.

You are so amazing; I pray I have done your namesake
characters justice. Thanks for letting me use you as inspiration
for a love story.

I love you.
Mom

Dear Reader,

Bringing you *Bridge of Gold* is a thrill. Several of my first published books were contemporary suspense—and I've written umpteen historical novels with suspense—but I had no idea how much I would love combining the two genres in a dual timeline. I'm sure I will write more in this genre!

I love these characters and the story. Since my daughter and son-in-law got married in 2020 and it was such a blast watching their love story unfold, I asked if I could use their names for characters in this story. They gave their permission, so of course I have a special love for their characters. (While there are a few personality traits and cute things throughout the story inspired by the real Steven and Kayla, please know that the characters in *Bridge of Gold* are still very much fictional.)

While I used the true events of the gold rush of 1849 and the building of the Golden Gate Bridge, another thing to remember is that this story, the characters, the ship, the mystery around it, and the treasure are all fictional (except for the historical people mentioned in the celebration ceremony—that is, the mayor and president). Any resemblance to real people is strictly coincidental. I let my imagination run wild while basing the story on as much historical fact as possible.

Researching the building of this historic bridge completely sucked me in. I even read a long dissertation written by Richard Thomas Loomis for his doctorate of philosophy from Stanford University. (You can access it here: https://www.goldengate.org/assets/1/6/loomis_dissertation_1958.pdf).

The most interesting area of research, however, was learning about the divers. Even with all our modern technology, diving today in the tumultuous strait is challenging. But to dive back then—before self-contained air tanks were invented? When their helmets alone weighed at least thirty to forty pounds? I can hardly imagine what it must have been like.

Another fun piece about this story is the crazy history of San Francisco. When I wrote *The Golden Bride* for Barbour a couple of years ago, I had the best time researching early San Francisco. I have to stipulate that I would not have wanted to live in San Francisco during its birth, but it is a fascinating era to research nonetheless. One of my favorite things was a map I found from National Geographic that shows all the ships from the gold rush that are actually underneath the streets of San Francisco. Hundreds upon hundreds of ships were abandoned by captains and crews so that they could all hunt for gold. Ships were dismantled, burned, sunk, and yes, even built upon.

The things I learn as I'm researching always blow my mind. For every book I write, I discover at least one fascinating fact that makes me even more curious to dig further. In this case, I was neck deep into researching San Francisco and the gold rush of 1849 when I discovered just how much the city expanded its borders beyond the original peninsula. In the back of my mind, I knew that I had heard or learned somewhere that the great Golden Gate city had built some of its streets on "landfill," but that was the extent of my knowledge. Then I discovered that this land growth started all because of the 1849 gold rush when a mass of ships came into the harbor. Day in and day out, ships were stacked into the small bay and cove. Hordes of men were aboard, all seeking their fortune, and many of those ships were abandoned. *Many* might even be too tame a word. *Most* is probably more accurate.

Some of those ships were torn apart to build makeshift buildings, while others were used to basically fill in the bays with whatever else they could find, and the peninsula's shoreline began to grow. To this day, quite a few ships remain underneath the streets of San Francisco. (Here's the map I mentioned earlier in case you want to check it out: https://www.nationalgeographic.com/news/2017/05

/map-ships-buried-san-francisco/). Never would I have guessed the last time I was in San Francisco that I was walking above ships from 1849. Talk about fascinating history!

If you're also intrigued by the notion of a city being built on landfill, check out this map from the Smithsonian, in which you can see the original shorelines compared to today: https://www.smithsonianmag.com/history/what-did-san-francisco-look-mid-1800s-180947904/.

I hope you enjoy the journey with Margo, Luke, Kayla, and Steven, and that your love of reading, story, and history is enhanced by *Bridge of Gold*.

Grabbing onto *joy*,
Kimberley Woodhouse

Chapter 1

Margo
February 26, 1933
San Francisco

Certain moments in life define a person. Moments that invoke physical feelings that can't be described. That flood the heart and soul with more emotions than could possibly be fathomed.

This was one of those moments.

Margo Hunley had a question to answer.

Her answer to Luke Moreau would change her life forever.

The scent of the salt water mixed with popcorn and the remnants from their picnic lingered in the air. Smells she would remember for the rest of her life.

Music and cheers from the celebration happening below them at Crissy Field made her smile. Very appropriate for today. The breeze picked up and made her skirt wrap around her legs.

Margo gazed down at Luke. So handsome in his black pinstriped suit, he was down on one knee and smiling at her as if the moon and stars obeyed her every whim.

"Well? Are you wishing me to ask again?" He winked at her.

She placed a hand on his cheek as her answer bubbled up inside her. "Yes!" She'd dreamed of this day since she was a little girl.

He jumped to his feet and threw his arms around her.

"Of course, I'll marry you." She laughed against his ear. "You know I've been waiting *ever* so patiently for the past two years."

Tipping his head back, he laughed. "I do know, *mon amour*. And it has taken me that long to save enough for your ring." He tapped the tip of her nose with a finger. "But it was not until I gained this job that I knew I could provide for you and a family." He pulled her close against him again and then stepped back and gripped her hands as his eyes sparkled. "Our dreams are all about to come true." Leaning in close, he captured her lips with his own, and she melted at his touch.

His French accent was one of the things she'd loved most about him from the moment she met him. And not just the accent but his voice. The sincerity and honesty that she always heard there. Luke had never once been false with her. And when he used his pet name for her—*my love*—it made her feel prized and adored.

Times had been tough since the Depression began, but they'd worked, scrimped, and saved so they could have a future together. Always dreaming and planning. Hoping for the day when their time would come.

Working on building the new bridge would be exactly what they needed for stability. His many odd jobs and her nanny position up to this point hadn't been enough for them to put much back, and worry had begun to creep in that the hardships would last for years to come.

But God had provided once again.

The sounds from the celebration drifted up to her in another wave of joyfulness.

Luke wrapped his arms around her waist as they watched from the hill above. "History in the making. What a privilege that we get to be part of such a day."

Even after the parade up Market Street and groundbreaking ceremonies, the huge crowd still hung around. "It is." Her smile widened. "It was fun to hear Governor Rolph and Mayor Rossi make their speeches, but to hear the telegram from President Hoover read? I think that was the most exciting. Something to tell our children and grandchildren about." She turned in his arms to face him. "Thank you for bringing me up here for a picnic. It's nice to have this time together. First to celebrate the bridge. Now to celebrate us."

He kissed her forehead and pulled her into another hug. "I love you more than life itself, Margo." His breath against her ear sent a little shiver up her spine.

"I love you too."

They stood for several moments. Simply watching the happiness below them. Margo's heart felt like it would burst.

There was much to look forward to.

Not only was the bridge over the Golden Gate Strait much needed, but it brought something even more important at this time: jobs that infused the community with hope. Hope that hadn't been present for a long time. No wonder the huge crowd had assembled and stayed. Everyone wanted to hold on to the feeling of hope and celebration for as long as possible.

As the joyous sounds washed over her, she looked back out to the water. She could barely imagine it—someday soon, a massive bridge would connect the two peninsulas. And now? She would be married before it was finished. She looked down at the delicate ring Luke had just placed on her finger. Maybe even their first child would get to see it completed. Lord willing, if He blessed them with children.

Warmth flooded her cheeks. They'd talked of family a lot lately. They both wanted a house full of children. The Lord would bless them with however many He saw fit. She hoped for five or six.

She tugged Luke's hand and pulled him back to the picnic blanket. The sun glistened off the waters of San Francisco bay as she sat down and arranged her skirt over her calves. "Come sit with me, Mr. Moreau. We need to plan our wedding."

"Of course, my love. Do we need to discuss dates? The sooner the better, if I have a say in it. We do not need anything fancy." He wiggled his brows, and it made her giggle.

"Yes. A summer wedding would be lovely, don't you think?" The colors over the water changed with the setting sun. She reached for her sketch pad. It was the last one her father had bought her before he died. Most of her pencils were nubs now, but she would use them until they were gone. And maybe one day she could buy new ones.

All her life, she'd journaled her emotions and thoughts with art. Not only was it a good way to keep her hands busy, but it helped her work through her feelings since she wasn't the best at talking about them.

"Whatever you desire, *mon amour*. Just tell me when and where. I will show up in my suit and declare my love to you for all time."

His words made her heart do another flip. To have the love of such a man. How did she get so lucky? "I adore you, Luke. Don't ever stop being the admirable man that you are." She gazed at him, loving the look in his eyes.

His eyes darted to her sketchbook with a knowing smile. "Draw me the sunset. . .please? So we may remember this moment always. It is worth the use of paper, *oui*?"

He always knew what she needed. Always encouraged her in her art. Supported her. Never once said it was a waste of time.

"I'd love to." She turned back to the pad in her lap.

"You inspire me to be a better man every day, love." He squeezed her hand and then snuggled up behind her and peered over her shoulder.

"This is a moment I want to savor—for the rest of my life. You definitely picked a great day to propose." She couldn't stop smiling. "Celebrating the bridge, and your new job. . .and now, *us*."

"I will remember this always. New beginnings all around. I wish to shout it where the whole world hears." He leaned in and kissed her cheek. "One day, Margo, I will build you that big house we've dreamed about."

"That overlooks the water?" She couldn't look away from the scene before her. Already she was envisioning how the sketch would take shape.

"Yes. And it will have a big porch."

"With rocking chairs. And a big kitchen?"

He chuckled. "Yes, and a *huge* kitchen where you can bake and cook to your heart's content."

"And I will learn how to make *croissants*." She made sure to say it like he did—*kwa-sons*—because she loved how it sounded. The French language was so beautiful. She wanted to learn it fluently so she could help teach their children one day.

He let out a little groan. "I will love you for it. Then I will grow round in my old age from all your marvelous cooking."

She glanced over her shoulder at him. "It's hard to imagine you growing round, my dear. You are strong but very thin."

"Wishful thinking. I remember my *grand-père* growing softer and rounder as he aged. It was comforting to sit on his lap and be held by his giant arms that had worked so hard." He laid his chin on her shoulder. "I can imagine raising our children here some-day. We can point to the bridge and tell them we were a part of its beginnings. That it was part of *our* beginnings because you said yes. . .today. We got engaged right here."

"You're such a romantic. You'll be the best father and will tell them amazing stories." The picture in front of her emblazoned in her mind, she began to sketch. Her hand moved swiftly over the paper as she penciled in the rough outlines. The rocks and cliffs. The edges of the foamy water.

His hand came up and brushed a few stray hairs behind her ear. "Yes." He chuckled. "I will tell them amazing stories, and you will teach them to draw amazing sketches and paintings. I love to watch you create. You are a true *artiste*."

"God is my inspiration. He's the best artist I know. I simply do my best to capture His creation."

"You tell a story with each picture. I love that. One day I will be able to buy you all the art supplies you need. Your art needs to be seen. Your heart is behind it."

"You bless me with your words, Luke. Thank you for believing in me. You know they say a picture is worth a thousand words—maybe they will be able to know even more of our story by seeing these sketches."

He wrapped his arm around her shoulder. "Our story. I like the sound of that. I will write it in French, and you will capture it in your beautiful drawings. Our. Story."

"It does have a nice ring to it, doesn't it?" Margo let out a long sigh. Could she be any happier than at this very moment? "You have such a way with words, Luke. I love seeing the pages you write and love hearing you read them to me. Although I can't read it myself yet, it's beautiful and something I know our children will love."

"Our children. That is something I love to hear. We will pray for the Lord to bless us with many children."

His words made her blush again. "I think I will title this picture *Beginning*. How do you say that in French?"

"*Debut*."

"Debut," she repeated. "I like it." As she worked on the sketch and then filled it in with color, the celebration began to quiet down. It was the perfect ending to a perfect day. The first day of the rest of their lives.

Luke
March 1, 1933

The dive suit was bulky and heavy, but as they placed the large, round metal helmet over his head and began to latch him in, Luke was thankful for the protection. The sea was turbulent. Currents from the Pacific pushed into the strait while the San Francisco Bay, with all its freshwater streams and rivers dumping into it, pushed back in a violent tug-of-war. Four times a day they had a scant twenty-minute window to dive when the tides were just right.

The only way the Golden Gate Bridge would get built was if they were able to build the south tower. But that meant they had a lot of underwater construction to do.

Stewart tapped Luke's helmet, and Luke gave him a thumbs-up signal. The hose that provided his air from the surface clicked into place. It was almost time for him to go. He stepped up onto the metal plate on the large steel swing that would lower him into the water.

Thoughts of Margo swirled in his mind. She'd said yes! The weight of the past few years and all its dark and depressing circumstances were washed away with the simple thought of her. How blessed he was to have her love and devotion.

He couldn't help but grin wide inside his dive suit. No matter what happened, he would always have Margo.

Another tap to his helmet drew his attention upward. The look on Stewart's face made Luke chuckle. Since he'd told the other guys this morning about his proposal, he'd been teased incessantly about wiping the smile off his face.

But he'd better focus now. The job demanded every bit of his attention. After days of this work, he'd gotten used to the rhythm but not to how difficult it was to see underwater. Gratefulness for his sight flooded through him. Visual cues and reminders were a part of every aspect of life.

The strong current constantly swirled dark silt. Even with the lights on their suits, the murky water made him feel like he was blind most of the time. A couple of the men had not been able to handle the conditions and asked to work elsewhere. But Luke was determined to do his best. Whether he could see or not. The job needed to be done.

A bell dinged. Time to go under.

As he was lowered into the water, he focused on what he needed to accomplish in the next twenty minutes. Several other divers were going down to the hundred-plus-foot depth so they could make the most of their tiny window. The charges were going to be set over the next several weeks to finish clearing the area they needed for the base of the south tower. Everything had to be in place for it to work.

But the water was different today. Pushing and pulling him on the heavy metal swing. As he gripped the large chain through his gloves as tight as he could, he closed his eyes and focused on his breathing until he felt the swing touch the seafloor. Working so close to the cliff underwater where the depth of the strait plummeted was a very real danger every diver was aware of. Not being able to see made the fear of going over the edge even more intense. Falling off the edge would bring disaster and death. The weight of their suits would take them to a depth no man could survive.

But Luke clamped his jaw, took a deep breath, and went to work. He fought with every muscle in his body against the water's surge to keep in the correct place.

Every once in a while, the current cleared the water a bit and he could see farther than just a foot or so in front of his face. But it didn't last long. He'd learned to be alert and ready when it happened so he could gauge his surroundings. Their lights couldn't cut much in the dark at this depth.

He set another charge and fought against the strength of the water. At this rate, it would take them a long time—probably longer than the scheduled timeline—to get the seafloor cleared enough to build the tower walls. Once the walls were above the surface, they could drain all the water out and build the rest of the massive, towering structure. The engineering was brilliant, but the hazards of nature were fierce. The designers knew some about the conditions and had planned accordingly, but it hadn't been until the workers began the project that they discovered what a challenge the construction would be. The north tower was well underway, while the south tower would take many more months to complete.

Out of nowhere, he felt like he was being pushed. As if the water had turned into a giant arm and was shoving him against the push of another giant arm. He felt the pull on his air hose as the water moved him farther from where he started. The water swirled and was too dark for him to be able to see anything. How far would it take him?

In that next instant, his feet gained the bottom but then slid. He was going over the edge! Grabbing at anything with his hands, he was slammed against something hard. He held on to the underwater cliff for dear life. He braced himself with his feet and arms, hoping that when the force of this current shifted he would be able to push off and have enough momentum to swim up and over the edge back to safer footing. Then he'd have to make it back to where he'd been working and find the lift swing.

In that moment, the water cleared and his light glimmered off something in the wall before him.

No. It couldn't be. His heart was racing from his precarious position. He must be seeing things. He blinked to clear his eyes. Breathed deep several times to calm himself. Waited for the water to clear again.

There it was.

Gold.

No matter how many times he blinked, his light glimmered on the object.

Using his bulky, glove-covered hand, he clawed at the piece until it came free. He gripped it tight. A bit smaller than a golf ball, this was no tiny nugget. Where had it come from? Could there be more? What was down here that would have gold? Treasure hunters had scoured the waters for decades with very little to show for it. Surely there wasn't anything left. It must be something else. Just a rock. Or something manmade.

But what had made it shine in the light? And where had it come from?

The surge of water from behind him decreased, and before he knew it, the flow shifted and he was being shoved in the other direction and up. For a split second, the water was clear and his light made the picture in front of him distinct. The outline of a ship.

He blinked. It was gone. The water was once again too dark and cloudy to see through.

Working with the current, he kicked his legs and swam as hard as he could, trying to get up over the ledge.

A tug on the hose aimed him back in the right direction. His time was up. He had to make it back to the swing so they could lift him back to the surface. The ride up was slow so the divers would be able to handle the adjustment in pressure as they rose from the depths and not develop bubbles of air in their brains. The fear of every diver.

Making his way back to the swing, his thoughts went back to the cliff and the ship. Maybe he'd dreamed it. His brain could have made up the silhouette he'd seen. Hadn't the doctor warned them of such things happening while diving?

As he crept toward the surface, he closed his eyes for a few seconds and took long, deep breaths. Then he opened his eyes, brought his hand close to the window in his helmet, and looked at what he'd carved out of the wall.

His heart beat faster in his chest. This could change everything for him.

Gold. He'd found gold.

The Son
March 2, 1933

Once the diving began, every day that passed was another day that someone else could get their filthy hands on what was rightfully his.

He narrowed his eyes and stared at the work going on down below him.

There had to be a way to keep that from happening.

He'd been combing the bay for months and hadn't been able to find it. Maybe the divers wouldn't find it either. They were focused on their jobs.

But what if the construction ruined it? They were setting charges after all. Intent on blowing up the bottom of the bay so the stupid tower could be built for the crazy bridge. His anger burned, and he slammed a fist into the tree beside him.

If only he'd been able to find it before the construction began. He'd thought he'd given himself plenty of time. But the blasted ocean didn't cooperate. No wonder it hadn't been found before now. Who could deal with the tides and currents in the dangerous strait?

Only someone determined.

Like his dad.

He pulled the tattered letter out of his pocket.

June 1, 1894

Dearest Agnes,

I found it. My fortune.

All the gold we could ever want. And it's all mine. As soon as I get it out from its watery grave, I'm coming for you and our son. There's no need for us to be apart any longer. You'll see. Everything will work out.

Your pa said that I would never amount to anything, and you'd begun to believe his poisonous words. Well, I'm proving him wrong. You'll see. And then you will want to come back to me.

You are my wife. You belong with me. I'm coming soon, and I will give you everything you've ever wanted. Watch for me. Give the boy my love, and tell him his pa is coming back for him. Just like I said I would.

Leo

The letter had come on his birthday. While his mother read it to him, she had shaken her head. She said they couldn't believe anything his dad wrote. That he never followed through with his promises.

But this one had to be true. It had to. Because Pa had gripped him by the shoulders and looked straight into his eyes before Mom dragged him away. His tone was adamant. "I'll send for you. Just you wait. We're family, and we're meant to be together."

No more than a week later, they'd gotten word that his dad had died when his horse threw him. Pa hadn't been able to finish what he had set out to do. But he'd found it. His pa had found it—he just hadn't gotten it out of the sea.

Mama moved on. They'd lived a miserable life. And all those years he'd dreamed about his father's gold. It had taken him years to find where his father lived when he wrote the letter. When he figured that out, he tracked down his dad's former landlady. And wouldn't you know it, the woman had kept a few things just in case family ever showed up. Good woman.

It was all he needed to finish what his father started.

But he'd run out of time. The stupid bridge builders were out there working constantly.

Somehow he needed to stop those divers. Just for a little while. Until he found what was his. Then they could blow up the whole strait for all he cared.

He'd have his gold.

Dad hadn't really abandoned them. He hadn't been as mean and angry as Mama said. He simply was frustrated with how hard his life was. That was all.

The gold would fix everything.

Chapter 2

Kayla
July 20, present day

Kayla Richardson looked down. She'd never lie, but she didn't want to answer her counselor's question either. A few strands of blond hair were stuck to the sleeve of her black sweater. She pulled at them, rolling them into a loose ball.

"Your silence tells me you *are* still having nightmares." Dr. Krueger cleared his throat. "Any more panic attacks?"

She snapped her gaze to meet his. "No. Absolutely none."

He leaned back in his chair. The gesture was meant to make her feel more secure. Less threatened. Like when he asked her to call him Johnathon at their first session. But if he thought she was lying, he could tell her boss that she shouldn't dive. For the work she did, it was a threat to her unlike any other. Diving was her life. Her escape. A year and a half ago, she'd been benched eight long weeks. . .back when her life fell apart. And yes, she'd had a panic attack. No big deal. But what would she do if she didn't get the counselor's go ahead—his approval? More to the point, *who* would she be then? It was a nightmare that her boss now required the mental health checks. All because of her. She didn't need any more stress in her life.

He raised an eyebrow at her. No spoken question. But it was there—hanging in the air.

Kayla kept her eyes trained on his. "I promise you, there have been no more panic attacks." Johnathon wasn't a bad guy. The sessions were mandatory every three months, and she chose to come more often because she wanted to heal. Wanted to put the past behind her. Didn't that say something about her? If only she earned brownie points for that. Of course her counselor didn't say things that pressured her—she did enough of that on her own.

Breathe. One. . .two. . .three. No one was saying that she was in trouble.

He continued to watch her in that quiet, disconcerting way of his. Hair graying at the temples, he looked like an old college professor with his beard and round glasses. "I'm glad to hear that. Now what about the nightmares. Be honest."

She rubbed her forehead and sighed. "The nightmares still come. I keep seeing my mother and how she died. I want justice for her. I want her killer to be found—"

"You've got to stop this train of thought, Kayla. Your mother was killed in an accident."

Defiance rose within her. She stood and began to pace the room. Like her counselor, the room projected calm—the dusky blue walls, the cushy carpet, the soft lighting, and the neat desk with potted plants in one corner and family pictures in the other. No computer. No tape recorder. Nothing to make a person feel watched or analyzed. But whatever calm she'd felt a moment ago leaked from her soul like salt water dripping off her dive suit. "You say accident. I say drunk driver. Every witness said the car was swerving all over the road."

"What if that person was a diabetic? Or they were having a severe asthma attack? Or a heart attack? What if that person died that night too? Think of the family of that person. I'm not trying to minimize your loss, but you're only looking at it from your perspective. It might not have been a drunk driver. That's why it was labeled an accident."

She pinched her lips together. Every few months, Johnathon hit her with these what-if scenarios. She'd argue that the person who killed her mother was guilty of murder, that it was clearly a hit-and-run. The police never found an abandoned vehicle, and no one else was brought into the hospital—all of which counteracted her counselor's speculations.

But it had been eighteen months. Her convictions weren't getting her past the pain.

Kayla sat down, leaned back in the chair, and closed her eyes. It wouldn't do any good to get all riled up. It just made matters worse. "I want all of this to go away. I'm tired. I'm tired of being angry at whoever hit my mom. I am."

"I understand that. But it's not just the loss of your mom."

It's like he *enjoyed* stabbing her with the direct words. Over and over again. Straight in the heart.

"You want to remain angry at the person who hit your mother because you feel like they also killed your father."

She gripped her hands tight until she felt the sting of her nails pressing into her skin. "Isn't that fair? Dad's heart attack was clearly because of what happened to Mom."

"You know what my answer will be." He quirked an eyebrow at her.

Life wasn't fair. Something she understood better than most. Closing her eyes, she worked on the square-breathing technique he'd taught her to deal with the panic attacks. It helped in lots of other situations as well. Like now. When she felt cornered.

While she'd always been strong and independent, she really wasn't a pushy or angry person. Before her mother was killed, most people thought of her as easygoing. Happy. Fun to be around. But the feelings the loss had brought out in her had made her defensive. Often short tempered. And yes, if she was honest, she'd become obsessed with the search for her mother's killer.

But all that had changed. Right? She was actively working on it.

Trying to find herself again. Hoping that she wouldn't be all prickly and hard for the rest of her life. It wasn't who she was.

Letting out a long sigh, she looked Johnathon in the eye. "I need to be *me* again. I'm tired of hurting over her death and then my father's. I'm tired of carrying all this around like a huge boulder on my back."

"Then you've got to let it go."

Not what she wanted to hear. "You've said that so many times, I keep waiting for you to break out into that *Frozen* song." She forced herself to smile, praying a little levity would help.

"You're deflecting." His smile didn't make her feel any better. "And let's face it, when the nightmares come, you don't rest well. If you're not rested, it can affect your cognitive and reactionary abilities. *Especially* underwater."

Kayla leaned forward. His words hit their mark. "Of course I'm deflecting. Look at these bags under my eyes. Yes, I need sleep. I need the nightmares to go away." Because if she didn't get rest—and soon—she *would* have another panic attack. And if that happened, she'd bench herself before Johnathon had to say a thing. She'd never put another diver's life at risk. Not even to save a career she'd spent her life and a small fortune working for.

The doubt that crossed his face with her honest words made her rethink her response. "But rest assured, I do make sure to get in naps so that I'm fresh." She couldn't allow him to think she wasn't capable and prepared. "Yes, I need to let it go. . .but how?"

The wrinkles in his forehead relaxed, and he took a long breath. He tapped the desk with his pen and set it down. "It's not easy. You have to choose to."

Yeah, right. If Mom were still alive, she'd tell her to go see a pastor rather than a psychiatrist she'd looked up in the phone book. But she wouldn't have needed to, because she could have just talked to her mom. Her sounding board. Her best friend.

She'd never have gone to a counselor in the first place if it hadn't been required for her job. So out of a rebellious spirit, she'd found this guy. And while he was nice, a good listener, and probably very good at what he did, she was still stuck. "Sure. Choose to. Like I can just choose that I will be happy. Choose that my next job will make me rich. Choose to dream about cotton candy and unicorns rather than the horrors that come to me at night." The sarcasm dripped from her lips, but she couldn't help it. Who was this person she'd become?

"Don't get mad at me for speaking to you honestly. Yes, it's a choice. It's a choice to let it go, release it from your mind. Promise yourself that you won't allow it to make you angry anymore. It *is* mind over matter. But I can't do it for you. Only you can."

Instantly regretting her verbal tirade, she let out a long sigh. "I'm sorry for lashing out. It's my go-to mode when I feel threatened nowadays."

"I know." The soft look on his face made her feel uncomfortable because he knew more about her than most. Maybe he was right. Maybe she could just decide to let it go and be done with it. Could it really be that simple?

Her phone played the theme to *Phantom*—the ringtone she'd assigned to all the politicians and bigwigs she had to work with.

Johnathon raised his eyebrows.

"I know, I'm sorry." She leaned sideways and picked up her purse from beside the chair. "I must have forgotten to silence it."

He smiled. "Your choice of ringtone is amusing. Very ominous."

"*Phantom of the Opera* is my favorite musical." She gave a shrug. But when she saw who was calling, she winced at Johnathon. "Sorry. I have to take this." She swiped right instead of hanging up. "Good morning, Mr. Mayor. What can I do for you?"

Her counselor rolled his eyes and waved her on. At least he understood her job.

She held up her index finger and mouthed, *One minute.*

"Miss Richardson," the mayor's voice sounded odd. "I'm not catching you at a bad time, am I?"

There was only one answer to that, so Kayla sent her counselor an apologetic shrug, grabbed her purse handle, and stood. "No sir, of course not." With a silent *Gotta go* to Johnathon, she hurried out the door. Her appointments were booked for the next three months and his bills were automatically paid from her checking account, so what would it matter to him if she left early?

"I need you in my office ASAP. We found something. . .interesting." Giddiness. That's what made him sound so different. Usually he was appropriately bored, as any good politician should be.

"I'm on my way."

Twenty minutes later, she twisted her long hair into a messy bun as she walked to the mayor's office. Dealing with politicians had never been her favorite, but it had become her normal. She was named one of the best underwater archaeologists in the world a few years ago, which is what led to her current assignment in San Francisco. The bay's waters were full of ships dating back to the gold rush, many yet to be discovered. Politicians controlled those waters and the artifacts they contained, so she'd learned how to play the nicey-nice game with them while she was on dry land to get what she needed under the water. That was her domain.

She took brisk steps down the long hallways and straightened her visitor name badge. What was so interesting to the mayor? It couldn't be ship salvaging. She'd been reporting her findings to him for five years now, and he'd never varied from one of three responses: "Good"; "That's nice"; or "How much will that cost the taxpayers?"

Opening the massive door to the office, she pasted on a smile and her best privileged-to-speak-with-the-mayor face.

"Good morning, Miss Richardson." The mayor held out his

hand as he walked around the conference table.

"Good morning." After shaking his hand, she took the seat offered to her.

"I'll get right to the point." He waved to the rail-thin, older man beside him. "This is Mr. Arnold—special counsel to the mayor's office. We need you to sign a confidentiality agreement before we can discuss matters."

Okay. . .not unheard of in her line of work but not standard either. Taking a moment to breathe, she looked out the wall of windows in the room that gave a beautiful view of the Golden Gate Bridge and the sparkling water beneath it. She sat straighter in her chair, anticipation tickling the back of her neck

The lawyer handed her some papers. "We need you to sign here, here, here, and here." He flipped through the pages and poked every red arrow that said, SIGN HERE. Was there a single lawyer who didn't point out the sticky notes indicating the signature lines? None she'd met so far. But then again, they got paid by the hour, so redundancy was cash in their pockets.

She perused the document—pretty standard nondisclosure stuff—and signed before sliding the pages back to the lawyer.

The mayor stroked his goatee. "Have you heard the legend of the *Lucky Martha?*"

She raised an eyebrow. "I have. It was a small schooner that was said to be a poor man's ship. It left Yerba Buena and then sank somewhere out in the strait. All aboard were lost."

"So you are familiar with it. And do you know anything about the cargo it held?" That he phrased the last as a question told her more than he let on.

But—to play nice—she chose her words carefully. "If you're referring to the rumored gold, credible historians have all discounted it. No ship and no survivors means no way to corroborate." But her explanation had no effect. The mayor still looked like a little boy with a secret stash of candy. She shook her head. "Has someone resurrected the legend?"

"Even better. The ship itself has been found." The smuggest of smiles lit the man's face.

It made her sit up even straighter. "Oh?" A little spark ignited in her imagination. The ships from legends were always interesting finds. Even if there was never any treasure, it was sure to hold significant artifacts and history. That's what drove her—she was a bona fide history buff. It's why she went into archaeology.

But after all this time? No. It couldn't be true. Could it? Treasure hunters had searched for the *Lucky Martha* for more than a hundred years.

"I see I have your attention now." The smile stretched into a grin the Cheshire cat would have been proud of. "Our restoration team—the divers—found it a day or so ago."

"The crew working on the Golden Gate Bridge?" She'd heard of the team who'd been commissioned to check every inch of the foundations of the towers. Since the southern tower's base was underwater, divers had to work that side. A daunting job.

"The very same. But as you well know, those waters are dangerous and violent. Probably why it hasn't been found before now. Or perhaps the tide and currents have moved it over time. I don't know. But what I *do* know, is that I need the very best to salvage the ship. They haven't touched anything, but the head of the company was the one who found it, and he told me that there are artifacts we'd definitely want saved"—the politician looked positively giddy now—"as well as treasure."

"You can't be serious?" She blurted before her professionalism could stop it. "My apologies." Kayla took a deep breath. "Are you telling me that you believe the legend is true? There's gold aboard?"

"From what we can tell, yes." The mayor went back to the head of the table, reached down to the chair, and lifted a gift bag topped with an origami tissue paper boat. Waltzing back to her, he presented it like she was a child and he the benevolent Santa granting her Christmas wish. "Here's a small sample."

The theatrics were a bit beyond her.

She lifted out the formed tissue paper—some secretary or intern probably spent an hour folding it—and set it on the table beside her. Peering into the bag, she had to keep herself from gasping.

At the bottom of the sack lay a gold nugget the size of her palm.

"And to answer the question I see brewing on your pretty little face"—he rubbed his hands together—"yes, it's real. We had it appraised before we called you in. Since it's unrefined and was found from within the ship, our experts say it's from the gold rush era. Obviously, that's why you're here. I need the best to work on this."

Experts? If it was someone she trusted, she'd believe it. But at this point, she was still skeptical. At least until she saw it for herself. Leaving the bag on the table, she leaned back in her chair and crossed her arms over her chest. "Is this a treasure hunt for the city of San Francisco, Mr. Mayor?"

"Not at all, Miss Richardson." His chin lifted an inch. "This is a substantial find of historical significance for the whole state and, dare I say, the entire nation." If his chest puffed out much farther, he'd lose the already strained buttons on his pinstripe suit. "But that's why we need the confidentiality agreement. We don't want word to get out to the press before we are ready to release it. We also don't want any risk brought to you or your team as you recover what's down there."

She raised an eyebrow. He was *concerned* about workman's comp or getting sued. And the gold. Who could resist the lure of gold? Certainly not a man like him.

Hating that her thoughts took such a negative turn, she made herself paste on a smile. "Thank you for your considerate words,

Mr. Mayor. It is wise for you to keep the news under wraps for now. It would put a lot of lives in danger if people tried to dive and recover any treasure that's there. Not many people are capable of diving in the strait and keeping themselves from harm. It takes years of experience and training to be able to handle that kind of turbulence."

"Exactly my thoughts. I would hate to put anyone in danger." He lifted his chin even higher. "Once again, I'm grateful that we have someone of your caliber here."

"I appreciate your confidence, sir. While it won't be easy, I know I can handle it."

"I knew you could." He walked toward the conference room door, a sure sign the meeting was over. "I've set up a meeting for you and Mr. Michaels tomorrow. He's in charge of the restoration team. He'll take you down to where they've found her."

She stood. "I look forward to it, Mr. Mayor." Which was only half true. She didn't like having another diving team involved—hers was trained to perfection—but it would be exciting to see what was down there. Even if there wasn't any gold, uncovering the history was enough for her.

Steven

July 21, present day

Steven Michaels marked the tidal times in his logbook. Diving today should be good. As long as the waters weren't too turbulent. The breeze picked up and he looked at the cloudless sky. A beautiful sight for San Francisco since they'd had to deal with lots of clouds, fog, and drizzly days recently.

He checked his watch, then looked down the length of the pier. Danny was headed his way, and Tim's pickup just parked. No sign of a woman, though. Where was the archaeologist? She needed to arrive in the next few minutes so they didn't miss their best window with the currents.

When the mayor said he'd hired an underwater archaeologist that would be heading up the recovery of the ship Steven had found, he couldn't balk. He'd heard plenty about the woman's reputation.

Miss Kayla Richardson.

Not only was she an expert diver, but she was at the top of her field. But he had to admit that after finding the ship, he'd wanted to be a part of the project himself.

Shaking his head, he forced his thoughts back to the task at hand. His job was to help with the underwater restoration of the bridge. Not get in the middle of their treasure hunt. It was hard enough to get his guys to focus on the job.

The thought made him chuckle. Wasn't that the truth? The best divers were great at what they did, but most of the time it meant they were the wild and adventurous sort. Not the best group at focusing. Or sticking with jobs long term. Because they loved the thrill. They thrived on adrenaline rushes. It made a mess for him trying to keep expert employees for more than a few months, but he couldn't complain. Divers and their personalities came along with the trade.

"Morning, Boss." Danny's low voice was gravelly as he made his way to where the boat was tied. His dark brown hair was spiked on the left side and matted on the right.

"Just get out of bed?" Getting the guys going early was always fun.

"You know me. I don't do mornings very well." He took a sip of his coffee. "As soon as I finish this, I should be fully awake."

Steven laughed and directed a look at the quartet of coffee cups sitting on the pier. "I brought more, in case you guys need it." He waved at Tim. The man's blond hair stuck out in all directions, making him look the part of a surfer with his wet suit around his waist and his bare feet.

Tim had had many nicknames over the years. All having to do with the waves. If he wasn't diving beneath the water, he was surfing. And he looked the part. He was one of many employees Steven hired despite knowing they'd promise to work for six months but disappear the moment good waves appeared in LA or Hawaii. Even so, the guy had been faithful to work with him for a couple years—longer than everyone other than Danny. Just as long as he had plenty of vacation time.

Tim slapped Danny's shoulder. "What's up?"

"The sky, dude." Danny's dry reply was the same every day.

Steven leaned over to pick up the coffee carrier, handing the caramel macchiato to Tim and the straight black to Danny. He took the double-shot mocha for himself. "Thanks for coming, guys. I needed two up and two down today. Because if we need assistance and signal, we'll need one of you to head down. Keep an eye on the water at all times. If things start to shift rapidly, we need to know."

"Sure thing, Boss." Danny drained the coffee he'd brought and started in on the second cup. It was his one vice—the never-ending stream of coffee. Other than that, he was an ideal employee. He showed up on time, was careful with equipment, didn't push his air tank farther than he should, and had never flaked on a commitment in the five years he'd been on the job.

Steven took a sip of his own drink. If he could find two or three more like Danny and Tim, he could cut back to single-shot mochas once a day. "I've already checked the gear, but let's go over it again. We're using two of the new DPVs today."

The diver propulsion vehicles were smaller and slimmer than the ones they'd used before, which would be great. But how well they handled the strong currents today would be the real test. He and the guys took turns checking and double-checking every piece of equipment as they joked around, something Steven encouraged to build camaraderie in his employees. Tim had great potential. If he'd just settle into the diving jobs instead of chasing waves, he'd be a great addition to the team permanently.

"Steady and sure" was Steven's motto. He wanted to be reliable—to be counted on—and that meant he wanted employees who were the same. Ever since he was a teen, he'd planned for the future. Whatever God had for him, he wanted to be ready. To do that, he had to be a good steward, plan, and realize that the race of life was often turtle paced.

If he could just teach Tim and Danny that. Watching his guys made him grin. They were good guys. And he trusted them.

Danny poked at Tim's blue T-shirt. "Wear that again and I'm gonna start calling you *Smurf*."

"Good morning, gentlemen." A soft voice interrupted their laughter.

Whoa! Steven jerked upright, slopping coffee across his wrist. All eyes shifted to the blond woman with her gear slung over her shoulder. How had she snuck up on them? He cleared his throat and stuck out his hand. "Steven Michaels. Good morning."

The lady smiled, her blue eyes observing them. "Kayla Richardson. It's nice to meet you."

He nodded in return. "This is Tim and Danny. They'll be staying up top while we dive. If we need assistance with anything, Danny will be ready to come down."

She turned toward them. "Good to meet you both. Thank you for helping today."

"Not a problem." Tim eyed the woman from head to toe, a flirtatious grin on his face. Always the lady's man.

She ignored it and turned back to him. "The mayor had great things to say about you, Mr. Michaels."

"While I appreciate it, we all know he's just excited about the ship I found."

She tilted her head back and forth. "True. But you know he

only likes to hire the best. So there's that." She slid all her gear to the dock.

Her attention away from him, Steven sized her up—purely for work purposes. Dressed in her dive suit, she was a good half foot shorter than his six-foot-four height. Slim. Broad shoulders. The look of a swimmer.

Her blond hair—wow was it long!—was pulled back into a thick french braid. As she bent down to work on her equipment, it swung over her shoulder. Her hair was thicker than anything he'd ever seen before and appeared to be trying to escape its confines. Wondering what it must feel like, he ran a hand over his own shaved head. The lady had some hair.

But it was her face that drew him in. Her eyes—a beautiful light blue—appeared guarded. Maybe it was simply keen observation— or the fact that she had to work with his crew today. He could imagine what his guys looked like to an outsider.

"My assistant, Carrie, needed the day off today, so I'm glad your crew was available. Thank you, guys." She made sure to send a smile to each one of them and then looked back to Steven. "Care to catch me up on what you've discovered, where the difficulties are that we might face, and anything else that would be crucial before we head down?" She pulled out her gloves and began to put on her gear without hesitation.

"The ship is about 120 feet down in the wall near the south tower."

"Over the edge?" She pulled on her flippers.

"Yep. Just over. The drop-off is pretty intense, and the water gets even stronger, as I'm sure you are well aware. We'll probably need to use our DPVs quite a bit. Mud and silt from all the currents over time have buried the ship almost completely. Visibility is about two feet at best when you can see through. There will be quite a fight with the shifting water. It's right in the flush area. If we get pushed too far one way or the other, we'll just use the props to get back to the site. We're also bringing down an anchor and guide rope that we hope to secure down there. That will make it easier to guide us back and forth. Otherwise, you know how hard it is to miss the tidal windows—we can't see our hands in front of our faces."

"So you're saying this will be quite the job." The grin that filled her face showed her enthusiasm for the project ahead. At least she wasn't one to get scared off easily.

"Yes. It's not like the ship is just on the ocean bed. It's going to have to be dug out. Very carefully. And unfortunately, the waters in the strait won't cooperate."

She quirked an eyebrow. "The strait isn't known for the best diving conditions. Probably why the ship hadn't been excavated before now. How much work do you all have to do on the restoration?"

"My bid was for three months, to be safe. I was hoping it would only be two, even with the dive windows being so short. But now with the ship being found, some of our work is going to have to wait."

"I can imagine." She finished her gear and adjusted her mask. "Let's go over our signals for while we're down there. I don't imagine I'll need a lot of time today, but I do need to see what we're dealing with so I can make a plan."

Danny handed her an extra flashlight. "How soon do you expect to start working on it?"

She tilted her head left and right again as she seemed to weigh it all in mind. "I probably need a week or so to get my team together and make a plan. Will that interfere with what your team is doing?"

"Not at all. In fact, we're fine if you want to schedule dives at the same time as we are working. It's a bit safer for everyone."

After going over their signals, they all climbed into the boat and sped out to the buoy that marked their dive spot by the southern tower.

As soon as they were anchored, she jumped into the water. "I'm ready when you are." She placed her regulator into her mouth and adjusted her mask. All business.

He liked it.

Steven jumped in, got his regulator adjusted and gave his team a thumbs-up. He looked over to Kayla. She gave him a thumbs-up, and he dove under the water, leading the way to their find.

It was a good thing the coordinates had been recorded exactly, because it would be easy to get twenty to thirty feet off in the clouded, shifting waters.

But as they made their descent, he had to use all the strength in his legs to kick himself toward their target. Even with the DPV, it was a workout. The quiet of the water gave him a sense of peace. Even the dark couldn't take that away.

As they came closer to the thirty-meter mark, all light was gone except for what they had from their flashlights. They both had one mounted above their masks and one in their belts as a backup.

At the moment they hit the ocean floor, the water inexplicably calmed for a moment and their lights picked up the edge of the cliff. Making their way to the edge, they moved slowly together and went over. Then his light shone on the outline of the ship in front of them. He pointed to make sure she saw it.

She kicked her feet to get herself closer, and he stayed back a few feet to watch. Her awe was clear. The same feeling overwhelmed him. To see something from the era of the gold rush was hard for him even to imagine. Times like these made him wish he'd gone into the same field as Kayla.

Her hands went to the structure in front of her. Starting at what appeared to be the bow of the schooner, she ran her hands along the wall and inched her way to the stern. He followed in her wake, marveling at the picture before them. He hadn't gotten this good of a look the other time he'd seen it. The waters had been too turbulent. But for the moment, they had the perfect view.

She turned her face back to him, and he saw the smile in her eyes. No longer guarded, they were lit up with what appeared to be excitement.

She loved what she did. That was apparent.

Covering the length of the ship twice, she never took her hands off the wood. When they made it back to the center of the ship, she stopped. Waved him closer.

Steven kicked his fins and came up next to her.

She pointed.

Following her finger, he got his face as close as he could. Was that. . . ? No. It couldn't be. But as he put his hand on it and rubbed away the mud, his light reflected off a discolored white bone.

A large one.

He glanced at her. Kayla's eyes were wide.

They signaled to each other and began gently digging around the remains with their glove-covered fingers. When it came loose, Kayla handed it to him.

A human bone. At least it seemed to be. Nothing he'd ever held before in his hands. It felt eerie. Weird.

He looked at her, but she was already digging at something else. The water became cloudy. Several moments passed. He kept squinting to see what she'd come upon.

The water swirled, stirring up dirt and debris so thick he couldn't see an inch in front of his mask. He shouldn't move, but where was Kayla? He reached out with one hand to see if he could find her.

A bump on his leg made him look down. The water swirled again, clearing his vision. She was tangled up in something and her arms were flailing. All skilled divers knew not to panic. But something had clearly upset her. He tucked the bone in his belt, reached his right hand down to her, and lowered himself to where she was struggling.

Then he saw it.

An entire human skeleton wrapped in heavy chains. And it was tangled around her legs pulling her down. And him too. A few more meters and they'd be too deep. They weren't geared up for a depth past 130 feet. She signaled for help.

In an instant, he went to work and realized her arms weren't flailing. She was trying to propel herself upward against the weight. The chains had snagged the DPV tethered to her waist, and she couldn't use it. When he couldn't get her untangled right away, he turned on his own prop, grabbed her arm, and kicked with all his might until they were up and over the underwater ledge. Once they could stand on the seafloor, he worked to free her from the chains.

When he got her clear, she signaled stop. But he signaled it was time to surface. She shook her head and turned away from him, working to get the chains free from the bones.

As an underwater construction diver, he cared about getting them back to the surface ASAP. Especially after that scare. His heart hadn't quite returned to its normal beat yet, and by the panicked looked he'd seen in her eyes a few minutes ago, hers had to be going a mile a minute too.

But she was an underwater archaeologist. This was her job. They had plenty of air and were no longer entangled and had made it to a safe depth. Of course, she would want to take her find to the surface.

But the chains were too well wrapped around the skeleton.

As they stared down at the remains in front of them, a thought hit him hard in the gut. Someone had wanted to make sure that whoever this was would never be able to get out. They must have been sunk with that ship. Or maybe the ship was sunk to hide the body. He couldn't tell which was true.

He got her attention. Now that she wasn't entangled, they could both use the DPVs to help them get to the surface with the extra weight. He signaled as much, and she nodded.

A few moments later, they headed to the surface. Him with a bone in his belt, and a chain-wrapped skeleton between them.

The mystery and legend of the *Lucky Martha* just got a lot more complicated. Because they weren't just dealing with an excavation. Now he was pretty certain they were dealing with murder.

Flip

July 21, present day

Flip rubbed a hand down his face. Things just got a lot more complicated.

No matter how hard he'd tried, he couldn't keep the divers away from the *Lucky Martha*. The ship was simply too close to the work on the south tower. Now that the city knew about it, the mayor was bringing in an underwater archaeologist. And she was good. He'd researched her last night online. Her résumé was long and without any negative marks. Not even one.

He'd watched them dive today.

There had to be a way for him to get the gold before they could get to it. Some way to delay everything. The *how* would be trickier.

Maybe he could damage equipment. Or get someone hurt if he had to. If he could get rid of the archaeologist, he'd buy himself a little time before they brought in someone new. But that might be too suspicious. What if he made things so difficult for her that she'd quit? It wasn't like there were a dozen underwater archaeologists just hanging around the unemployment office looking for work. Especially not when the mayor wanted the best.

Whatever Flip did, he needed to do it soon.

Accidents happened all the time. Besides, she appeared plenty shook up after the dive today. Perhaps he could use that to his advantage.

His mind circled back to the biggest problem. Too many people were in the know about the ship.

The mayor knew. Kayla Richardson knew. The whole crew of Steven Michaels Underwater Construction knew.

Silencing one person was possible. To silence them all? Impossible. Not without it pointing right back to him, and he wasn't going through the risk of getting that gold just to spend the rest of his life in prison.

Walking over to the wall beside the closet, he gazed at all the notes, maps, and pictures he'd hung up. Each one held clues and information that had helped him find the *Lucky Martha*. That ship was his. He deserved it.

It was really all about time. It wasn't a secret anymore.

Picking up the old journal, the pages yellowed and fragile, he opened it to where he kept the letter from the first man who'd found the schooner. Tucked between the pages, it was much older than the journal. The guy was a husband and dad. Wanted his family back. He related to the man more than he cared to admit.

Then there was the son—the one who wrote the journal. That guy wanted to believe in his father. It made perfect sense to Flip. He wanted his own family back. And finding the gold was the key for it to work. Setting the book back down on his bed, Flip shook his head. Other people were after what was his. And he had to stop them.

Focus. That's what he needed. Focus on the problem at hand.

He went over to his computer. Maybe he just needed to do more research on that pretty archaeologist. She had to have an Achilles' heel somewhere—something he could do to make her quit. What happened today could be the catalyst. He just needed a plan.

As he studied another article that shouted her praises, his computer pinged that he had a new email.

Switching tabs, he opened it up.

From his wife.

LEAVE ME ALONE.

WHY CAN'T YOU GET THE POINT? YOU'RE A LOSER. ALL
YOU'LL EVER BE IS A LOSER. AND I WON'T BE A PART OF
YOUR CRAZY DELUSIONS.

I DON'T WANT TO SEE YOU EVER AGAIN. DO YOU
UNDERSTAND ME? NEVER AGAIN. STOP CALLING. STOP
WRITING. STOP COMING BY MY WORK. WE ARE OVER.

I'M GETTING A RESTRAINING ORDER, SO UNLESS YOU
WANT TO BE ARRESTED, YOU'D BETTER LISTEN THIS TIME.

Flip slammed his computer closed. She didn't have the right. *He*
decided when, where, and how anyone said goodbye to him.

And whether it was temporary or permanent.

She'd eat those words.

They'd be back together.

Soon.

Chapter 3

Luke
March 10, 1933

No matter how much he tried to convince himself that keeping the gold a secret was a good thing, Luke was plagued by its existence—and the simple knowledge that he had discovered it in the first place.

He ran the length of the pier that led to their dive site to where the south tower would be constructed.

"You're late." George tucked his helmet under his arm. "Everything all right?"

"Oui. Yes." Luke hurried to get into his suit.

"It's a bad habit to put on your equipment without checking it first." His friend and dive partner tilted his head toward the helmet and air hose. "I, of course, checked mine. . .and yours." George elbowed him. "Do you trust me?"

Even though it was said in jest, it was the question that Luke had wrestled with since finding the gold. Who could he trust with the secret? Margo had questioned him not more than a half hour ago, refusing to accept that he wasn't hiding anything from her. For ten days, he'd kept up the charade, and it was eating him up inside. All because he couldn't make a decision about what to do. And truth and honesty had always been his priority. Something else that ate at him.

It had taken more time than he had and every ounce of his

persuasive powers to assure his fiancée that he was fine—that *they* were fine. Which was true. Except for the wretched gold.

Luke fastened up his heavy suit and secured the belt for the rope. "What are we working on today?"

"Same as usual. Preparing the seafloor for the forms."

Luke's heart bumped against his sternum. Every day they cleared more. More charges were set. Soon the forms would be laid. And not too long after that, they wouldn't be needing the guys to dive. Which meant he'd lose his chance to find the ship again.

He tried to get rid of the thought. Did it really matter? He hadn't even had the courage to find out if the gold was real. Each day, he'd gotten closer to speaking to George about it. Truly the only friend he could trust. Maybe his friend could help him decide what to do. The options he'd considered varied depending on his mood at the moment. But whether he searched for the ship again, sold the gold nugget, or tried to forget about it all together—one thing was all too clear. He couldn't keep this from Margo for much longer. It was eating him up. And anything was better than leaving the chunk hidden in one of his good church shoes and buried in his trunk.

The debate in his mind had become torturous. He needed to talk to someone about it.

"Ready to go?" George waved a hand in front of his face.

Luke focused on his friend. "Sorry. Oui. Ready."

"Keep your wits about you, my friend. I need you alert down there."

He nodded. George—a family man—took safety concerns as top priority. Luke couldn't ask for a better dive partner. He gave a thumbs-up signal as they were locked into their helmets. Determination filled him. When they came back up, he would talk to George and get it off his chest.

The gold could be a blessing from God. He'd prayed for help.

For rescue from these difficult times. This could be an opportunity to help a lot of people less fortunate with the money.

Decision made, he took long deep breaths and prepared his mind for the dive. Stepping onto the large swing, he prayed for safety.

Water rushed over his suit and helmet and closed like a window to another world. The feeling was always a bit surreal. The first few moments of a dive—adapting to the surroundings and breathing properly—were crucial. He glanced to his right.

George signaled to him from the other diving swing. They'd been working together the past week on every dive. The boss really liked them as a working pair because they'd been getting each job accomplished every dive. The success rate with the other divers was only about 75 percent.

The water seemed calmer as they reached the seafloor. He didn't have to use every muscle in his body to try and stay in one place, which was a welcome reprieve. George sent him a thumbs-up, and they went to work on the molds for the concrete. This area of the seafloor had already been cleared by charges and powerful hoses to make it level. They discovered early on that they had to place the forms as soon as things were clear, because the tides and currents could change the situation dramatically in just a few minutes' time. Then they'd have to blast and clear more area, set forms, and start over again. It was a taxing and long job. Especially when they had so little time to dive safely each day.

He'd only set three forms by the time his rope was tugged on, which was the signal that he had a minute to finish whatever he was working on. Then he'd be reeled in like a fish until they reached the metal swings, and from that point, he'd be lifted slowly to the surface.

As soon as his helmet broke the top of the water, Luke reminded himself of his plan. It would be a relief. Taking off the dive equipment could take up to an hour. An hour that gave him way too much time to think about it all over again.

"You've been awfully serious lately, Luke." George elbowed him. "Don't tell me that you're having second thoughts about marrying Margo. 'Cause if you are, I know a couple fellas who would love a chance."

His friend's teasing brought his head up. "No second thoughts here, my friend. Not a one. Margo is the best thing that the good Lord has ever given me." He smiled wide at George. "How is your sweet wife?"

"She's wonderful and as beautiful as ever." George winked at him. "Being married is way better than being single."

"I cannot wait for our wedding day."

"Then what's got you so glum lately?" George headed toward the lockers where they kept their personal things.

He shrugged. Maybe it would help to have someone to talk to. George was trustworthy—he trusted him with his life. They'd worked many jobs together over the past few years. They were in the same men's Sunday school class at church.

"I can tell that you're strugglin' with something." George sat on one of the benches. "Just remember that I'm here for you if you ever need anything."

Luke opened his locker and pulled out his street clothes. It would be nice to have someone help him with this burden. "I found something last week."

"Oh?" George laced his boots. "At your apartment?"

"No. Down at the bridge site. Underwater. When I was diving." How much should he say? A niggling at the back of his brain made him worry. But about what? George was his friend. "The current shoved me over the edge and up against something. Then I saw a glimmer. I dug it out and brought it to the surface. It was a nugget of gold. And when the water shifted directions, I was able to get a glimpse of what appeared to be the outline of a ship."

George's eyes were wide. He looked around them, then stood and grabbed Luke's arm. "Let's go outside."

"All right." Why was his friend being so squirrelly? He followed him out the door.

Glancing all around them again, George then whispered. "I don't think that's something you should be telling anyone else. Lots of men are struggling right now, and who knows what they would do to get their hands on some gold. Desperation makes men do strange things."

"I have not spoken about this to anyone but you. But it has been bothering me. Often I cannot sleep. What if I have stumbled upon some treasure? Do I have a right to claim it? And how am I supposed to find it again? The waters in the strait are very dangerous, and I do not own diving equipment."

With a nod, George crossed his arms over his chest. "I suggest that we pray about this and ask God for guidance. There's got to be a way we can rent some equipment, manage to get back down, and see what it is that you found. It could be that there's only the one piece that you found. Are you sure it was a ship?"

This was what plagued him the most. "I am not entirely sure. I was convinced at the time. But I only saw it for a brief moment."

"Can you show me the gold? Are you sure it's real?"

"I have it hidden. How does one go about finding out if it is real?"

George pursed his lips. "That, my friend, is something I don't know. But I guess we should find out."

Margo
March 15, 1933

The children had been a handful lately. Margo rubbed her forehead. Some days she loved being a nanny much more than others. She wasn't sure what had gotten into them, but hopefully they would get back to their normal, cooperative selves soon.

Maybe she could spare a bit of change to buy a headache powder. She desperately needed some groceries for the next few days. She could scrimp a little to be sure. . .because something had to help the ache in her head.

But then she had the dinner she planned to fix for Luke tomorrow night. And she'd really wanted to impress him with something more than just potatoes and soup. It had taken her a month to save enough from her meager grocery budget so she could buy a tiny amount of meat. Would there be enough for medicine as well?

Maybe she could simply deal with the headache. The meat was more important. It even made her mouth water just to think about it.

Entering the store, she pulled her list and a pencil stub out of her pocketbook. Her head throbbed, and she put a hand to her temple. She could add up each item as she put it in the basket, and if there was anything left, she might think about getting that powder.

Shopping at the market was a difficult challenge. Every woman weighed each choice with care. What would it be like to get past these tough times and not have to pinch every penny? It seemed like a dream. But she wasn't so young that she didn't remember what it had been like before the Depression hit.

Dreams had crashed along with the stock market. Jobs were lost. Homes were lost. Everyone was affected. At least everyone she knew. She heard about the wealthy and how they still lived with plenty. But she hadn't seen any of them. It must be a different world.

Even the people she worked for were struggling. Both parents had jobs. But she saw how little they had and how little food was in the cupboards. The Albrights were fortunate to have jobs for the two of them, but they scrimped along just like the rest of the world it seemed. Margo suspected they'd hired her out of the goodness of their hearts.

Many days she wondered if she would have a job from day to day. But she would be thankful for what she had. Many couldn't find jobs. There weren't enough for the huge number of people without work.

The store aisle was empty of shoppers. So sad. It had been such a bustling little market a few years ago. Not only were the shelves mostly bare, but the store was bare of customers. It made her want to weep and long for the days gone by. But that wouldn't do her any good. Best to be thankful for what she had and look forward to the future.

She was getting married. Smiling as she made her way down the aisle, she reminded herself of every good thing God had given her. People mattered. Relationships mattered. Not the amount of money she had in the bank or what size home she lived in. The little room she rented wasn't much, but at least it was a roof over her head. And she would be ever so thankful for that.

When she rounded the corner to the produce section, she gasped. The price of potatoes had gone up five cents for ten pounds! How could she afford that?

Potatoes had been the mainstay of her diet. Most people couldn't afford meat or many vegetables. Not unless they grew them themselves. But she didn't have that luxury.

Tallying her small basket so far, she checked to see how much there was to spare. She put a few potatoes on the scale.

Took one away.

Then another.

There. She could get by with those. Maybe. No headache powder today. Food was much more important.

Perhaps she should bake an extra loaf of bread to help stretch her meal with Luke. If she had to eat bread every day for the next week as her only sustenance, she would do it. Everyone had to sacrifice in these times.

But she did not want to sacrifice the money she'd carefully saved for the meat.

Walking to the butcher's shop, she carried her sack of groceries. It wasn't too heavy, especially not compared with the children she usually carried around during the day. But it had been a long week and the half mile made her shoes pinch.

A cool, salty breeze washed over her.

How she loved this area. San Francisco was beautiful. Always temperate. Hardly ever too hot and rarely too cold—almost always perfect. At least to her it was.

As she crested the hill, she caught a glimpse of the ocean. The magnificent deep blue made her wish she could sketch it with all the colors of the sky behind it. The clouds were tinged a pink hue with the sun behind them. It wouldn't be too long before sunset.

She needed to get home. It wasn't advised for single women to be out and about after dark. Not that she ever wanted to be. Unsavory characters thrived in the dark.

Fifteen minutes later, she exited the butcher's shop with her prized piece of beef wrapped in brown paper and tied with string. She tucked it into the bag of groceries so no one could see it. Not something she wanted to flaunt at the moment.

But oh, how marvelous it would taste. She and Luke would be able to savor their meal and enjoy their special time together. It made her think of the future when they would be married. They could share meals together every day. . .a home. . .and everything else. The thought made her blush and tip her lips up in a smile.

As she walked up the steps to the house where she rented a room, she got out her key for the door. Jiggling the knob as she turned the key, she balanced the sack on her knee. Once inside, she checked her box in the entryway and found a couple of pieces of mail.

She trudged up the stairs to her room, unlocked the door, and went inside. She placed the sack on the tiny table that wasn't even big enough for two and rolled her shoulders. Relieved of the burden, she looked to the mail.

A letter from her friend in Sacramento. The other bore only her name. Wonder who that could be from? There wasn't a stamp, so had someone brought it by?

Opening up the envelope, she stifled a yawn. Then she pulled out a small, torn sheet of paper and read:

> *Tell your boyfriend that if he knows what's good for him, he'd better quit his job and move out of town. I know what he has, and it doesn't belong to him.*

Chapter 4

Kayla
July 22, present day

She folded her hands in her lap and looked up at her counselor. "Whatever I need to do to get past this. . .I want to do that." After the nightmare last night, something had to give.

Johnathon leaned forward. "Why don't we start with whatever brought you in today for an extra session."

Kayla closed her eyes for a moment then snapped them open and sighed. She'd made up her mind to deal with this. "We had an interesting incident yesterday while diving." While she couldn't tell him the circumstances because of the confidentiality agreement she'd signed, she told him about the skeleton wrapped in chains, which led to the conclusion that the person had been murdered. And what that had brought up in her—anger, obsession over finding her mother's killer, frustration.

"I take it you also had another nightmare about your mother last night."

"Yes. But it went further. It morphed into the skeleton wrapped in chains. I was all tangled up, and it dragged me down." She didn't want to tell him about the panic attack she'd had after she'd woken up gasping for air. Not yet. But it had jolted her enough to ask for an appointment today.

"How did that make you feel?"

The question always made her want to roll her eyes, but she

refrained. "Scared. Obviously. But after some tea and the rest of a sleepless night praying and examining my life, I knew I had to truly let all of this go. I can't afford for this emotion and anger to rule my life anymore."

A sad smile lifted the corners of his mouth. "I'm really glad to hear you say that. That's truly the first step to recovery."

Two hours later, Kayla walked into the medical examiner's office and found Steven waiting for her. She forced a smile. The session with Johnathon had been good. She did feel better. But she longed for a decent night's sleep. Mind over matter.

Steven greeted her with a smile of his own. His at least looked genuine. "It sounds like they've got a lot of information for us." He tipped his head in the direction of the office.

They walked down the hall together, chitchatting about the weather.

She really should put in a little more effort. He was a good guy, as far as she could tell, and it wasn't his fault they'd found a skeleton that intensified her nightmares.

He opened the door to the morgue for her. No one had done that chivalrous act for her since her dad died. A strong, antiseptic smell filled her nose and made her eyes water.

"Martin, I'd like you to meet Miss Richardson. She's the underwater archaeologist I was telling you about." Steven looked at the ME.

"Please. Call me Kayla." She didn't hold out her hand in greeting since the man's gloved hands were inside a corpse at the moment.

"It's an honor to meet you. Your reputation is quite stellar." The medical examiner took his hands out of the chest cavity, looked up, removed his gloves, and walked over to the refrigerated locker drawers where the bodies were kept.

"Well, thank you."

He opened drawer 117. "I had to put the remains in here since we've been swamped. I didn't want anything to contaminate them."

Crossing his arms over his chest, Steven now looked all business. "What have you found?"

Martin lifted his eyebrows. His expression was practically giddy as he pulled out the tray and lifted the blue sheet covering them. "Fascinating stuff, I'll tell you. The bones. . .they don't belong to just one person."

"What do you mean?" She stepped closer.

"This bone over here is a tibia. And I already had two tibia bones in the skeleton, so I knew I was dealing with more than one person."

Okay then. She hadn't been expecting that.

The ME walked around the drawer. "Did you find the bones together?"

"We found the single bone first." She puzzled over the facts. What did it mean?

"They were only a few feet apart," Steven added. "I guess we both assumed they were all one. Are we looking at two murders then?"

Martin shook his head. "I can't speak to this single bone over here as to cause of death, nor could I definitively tell you that the intact skeleton was murdered—other than what you told me about the chains, which were a clear sign. But"—he pointed his finger at them—"the most interesting piece is that the skeleton is far older than the other bone."

She drew her brows together. "What are you saying? The person was older?"

"No. Well, I guess, yes, the person would be older than the other only because of the difference in years. Wait, that's not what I meant, was it? Let me try again. This person"—he pointed to the skeleton and pushed his glasses up the bridge of his nose—"died rather young."

"I'm sorry, I'm really confused." Kayla stepped even closer to examine the remains.

"All right, this person would be older, only because of when they were born, not by age of when they died. Sorry to confuse you. I tend to ramble when I get excited, and this case has resurrected the forensic scientist lurking inside me." The man's words came out faster and faster the longer he spoke.

"I'm afraid I'm still lost, Martin." Steven put his hands on his hips.

The man took a deep breath and put his palms on the table as if to calm himself. "The skeleton and the single bone are from two different time periods. Meaning, they went into the water decades apart. If my analysis is correct—I'll be double-checking the findings—this bone has been down there since around 1930—probably sometime around when the bridge was built. But the skeleton? It appears to be from much earlier."

"How much earlier are we talking about?" The archaeologist mind inside her went into hyperdrive.

"The skeleton appears to be from the 1890s."

Steven

Standing beside Kayla's blue convertible VW Bug outside the medical examiner's office, he fidgeted with his keys. When his team had come upon the *Lucky Martha* pretty much buried in the seawall, they had stopped all work on the restoration so they didn't ruin anything of historical significance. He never expected to find gold when he found the hole in the side of the ship. But he had. And if that hadn't complicated things enough, now there were human remains to deal with that revealed another mystery. Including murder.

"I take it from your silence that you're just as dumbfounded as I am." She tossed her bag into the back seat of her car.

He leaned his hip against her car. "I'm not even sure what to think." He swiped a hand down his face and watched her slip on her sunglasses. "It's not every day that I have to deal with human remains. It's a lot to process."

A half smile lifted her cheeks. "Finding bones isn't uncommon in what I do, but knowing there was a murder definitely is." A slight breeze lifted strands of her hair, and she ran a hand through it to get it off her face.

"Finding out the bones are from different eras must have that history-loving brain of yours working high speed."

She let out a light laugh. "Definitely. I mean, we knew the ship was from the gold rush time frame, which is of great historical significance. But with the discovery of the bones. . .and now with the info from the medical examiner"—she turned her face to look toward the bridge—"there's obviously a lot more to uncover. It's got to be a great story. Whatever it is."

"How long do you think it will take you and your team?"

Her brows lifted over the sunglasses, and she pursed her lips. "That is a really good question. I've got two divers on vacation right now. Which is long overdue. I wasn't going to pull them back just because the mayor requested my work on this job. Since it's just me and Carrie, I'm not sure I have an answer." With a grimace, she placed a hand on her hip. "That's going to drastically delay your schedule, isn't it?"

"Yeah. But that's all right."

"Maybe I could hire a few more divers. It's always a pain, but I'd be willing to do that so it doesn't affect you too adversely."

"Don't worry about us. And there's no need to hire anyone else. I already offered our assistance to the mayor when he told us to halt our work so we wouldn't damage the ship in any way. If you need help, my team is ready and willing."

With another glance out to the bridge, she was silent for several seconds. If only he could figure out what was going through that mind of hers. Then she turned back to him and stuck out her hand. "I would appreciate that, Steven. I know we don't have a lot of time to waste."

"Anytime." He shook her hand. "Why don't we go get a cup of coffee so we can discuss what to do next?" Kayla Richardson was a bit of a conundrum to him.

She removed her sunglasses and polished them on her shirt. "All right. I'll follow you?" Her blue eyes seemed darker in the cloud cover of the day. But then she put the glasses back on and it was like a curtain had closed.

"Sounds good. I'm in the black Expedition down the row." He jogged over to his SUV, climbed in, and started it. Backing out of the space, he watched in the rearview to make sure she was behind him. It was hard to miss her long blond hair over her shoulder. As she pulled up behind him, he noticed she held up a finger asking him to wait.

Watching in the mirror, he saw her twist her long hair round and round and then shove some kind of shiny clip into it. She smiled up at him and signaled she was ready to go.

The coffee shop was about a mile away, but traffic today—as usual—would end up making the trip about ten minutes. As he drove, his thoughts were on Kayla. Professional and very good at her job, she kept to herself. He'd researched her online. She was extremely intelligent and had finished grad school quite young. At only twenty-eight years old, she was at the top of her field and had been for several years.

The more time he spent with her, the more he realized he wanted to get to know her better. No woman had piqued his interest in quite some time. Probably because owning his own company took most of his time and energy. Or it could be because his standards were pretty high. Something his mom continually teased him about.

While Kayla was a natural beauty, it wasn't just her appearance that drew him. They had a lot in common from what he could see so far. Diving was just one aspect he admired. She'd used her popularity with the underwater archaeology crowd to raise money for underprivileged kids to learn how to swim and eventually dive. Even used her own vacation time to teach classes herself.

She'd lost her parents within the last couple of years, and it appeared she poured herself into her archaeology and charity work even more after the loss.

As everything he'd read about her raced through his mind, he mentally bopped himself upside the head. Nothing stalkerish about spending three hours researching her.

Maybe he should forget about everything that was on paper about the lady and actually get to know her. Today was a great start. They'd be working together for a while.

Miraculously, he found two empty parking spaces on the same block as the coffee shop. He took the one farthest from the door, got out, and locked his vehicle.

She parked in the slot next to him.

He waited for her to grab her purse and a backpack and then walked beside her, trying to shorten his steps to stay in pace with her. While she was probably five foot eight or so, the long legs carrying his six-foot-four frame ate up a lot more distance with each step. At the door, he reached forward and opened it for her.

"Thank you." Her eyes showed her surprise. But the smile that lit her face made him hope it was a good one.

After they'd ordered their drinks and taken seats at a high-top table out on the patio, Steven took a sip of his double espresso and looked at her over the top of his cup. "So what are your thoughts? You're the expert here."

She crossed her arms over her middle and leaned back against the chair. "You know, I'm like you. I'm not quite sure what to think either. I was hired to acquire the historical artifacts and any. . .objects of value down there."

He grinned. "Don't worry, I'm the one who found the gold, so I know what the mayor is all excited about."

Letting out a sigh, she looked relieved. "At least you know." Kayla put a hand to her forehead. "I'm not a treasure hunter—even though I feel like that's what the mayor is really after—but I'm willing to do the job because it holds a lot of historical significance. History has always been a love of mine." She pulled a couple of tattered books out of the backpack. "That's what got me into the field in the first place. I know a lot of people are purely after making a buck. But to me, I think we need to save as much of our history as possible so that future generations can learn about it and from it."

Her passion came out in her words, and it made him smile even bigger. "That's exactly why I do restoration. For instance, the bridge job. It's fascinating to me. To think that it was almost a hundred years ago that construction was started. And what the workers had to go through. I'm amazed."

She tapped the top book. "I've been reading up on it since taking the job. It still baffles me to think of what diving was like before self-contained air tanks were invented."

"It's definitely hard to imagine. The gear they wore weighed a ton. And having to rely on your air coming from the surface? That's the part that gets me."

"Oh, I can't even. . . I'm too much of a control freak to even think about that." Leaning back in her chair, she reached up and pulled the clip out of her hair. It tumbled around her shoulders.

She rubbed her scalp with one hand. "Some days it's too heavy to leave up. Especially when I have a headache." Taking a long sip of her Frappuccino, she squinted. "Today is one of those days."

"Yeah, I struggle with that too." He winked and ran a hand over his bald head.

She set down the cup and covered her laughter with a hand. "Thanks." Shaking her head, she lowered her hand. "I needed that laugh."

Watching her face relax, he wished they didn't have to talk about work. This was nice. "Happy to help. Although my mom reminds me that all my jokes are pretty cheesy. But she laughs anyway."

Sadness washed over her features, and she looked away and then down at her watch.

Something he said? He ran through their conversation and wished he could take back his words. He'd brought up his mom. Her mom had died recently. What a heel.

When she turned her head back, her eyes shimmered.

Great. He *was* a heel.

"I can tell by the look on your face that you know I lost my mom."

"I'm sorry, Kayla."

She held up a hand. "Don't worry about it. You didn't say anything wrong." She cleared her throat. "I need to get going in a little bit, so we should talk about tomorrow."

"Sure. Of course. What do you need my team to do?"

"I need to brief the mayor on what the medical examiner discovered, and even though solving a murder isn't what I signed up for, that does have bearing on how the excavation will go from here."

"What's the protocol in this kind of a case?" He leaned forward and put his elbows on the table, giving her his full attention.

"First, we have to discover if there are any more bones in the adjacent area. Human remains take priority over everything else. Then I'll have to carefully dig out from where we started and go from there. Since there may be clues to why that man was drowned, we have to be meticulous. I'm afraid this just slowed down my timeline a great deal."

He raised his eyebrows. "And you're worried about the mayor not liking that."

"Exactly."

"My team of guys is very responsible and trustworthy. Just tell us what to do and we'll do it."

Her shoulders relaxed a bit. "That will be a huge help. As long as they listen to instruction. It's not a piece of cake doing an archaeological dig underwater. Especially in the waters in the strait."

"Tell me about it. Everything we've done so far took at least three times as long as normal. But my guys are great. They can handle it." He watched her face as she looked out the window and blinked several times. Taking another sip of his coffee, he waited while she processed.

She looked back at him. "I don't want to push you, but I'd like to get down there again ASAP and see what else we can find. If we have to wait awhile for Martin's findings to be verified, I'd like to see what else I'm dealing with."

Even without a bit of makeup, the woman was beautiful. But he doubted she knew it.

She pulled a notebook and pen out of her bag. It took her a moment to flip through several pages, and then she stopped and studied it for a moment. The pen tapped against her lip. "My initial list will have to wait until we clear up whether there are more remains down there, and that could take a good while." Looking back into his eyes, she raised her eyebrows. "How soon can you brief your team and get them ready for a dive?"

"I can have them ready first thing in the morning."

With a nod, she smiled. "Perfect. Let's meet at 7:30? I'll need to give them quite a bit of instruction before we go down. You'll have guys to stay topside?"

"Sure thing."

"Great, because I need my assistant with me to help show your guys where to go." She glanced at her watch. "I've got to go brief Mr. Mayor on what's happening." She rolled her eyes. "But thank you for this. I was beginning to think I was in over my head, so having an experienced team of divers to help will be incredible."

"Not a problem. We're glad to help. I'll see you in the morning." He stood as she got up, gave him a brief smile, and then headed for the door. As much as he wanted to think about how interesting Kayla Richardson was, he needed to round up his guys and tell them to be ready for another early morning.

One he wasn't going to mind one bit.

Chapter 5

Margo
March 15, 1933

Shivering in her thin sweater as the fog rolled in over the inky sky, Margo knocked on the door of the house where Luke rented a room. Prayerfully he was off work and home so they could talk, because she wouldn't be able to eat or sleep until she found out what was going on. The note had shaken her up more than she wanted to admit.

The door opened a crack. "Miss Hunley." The older woman who owned the house lifted her chin, her gray dress making her look even more sour. "It's awfully late for you to be visiting."

"I'm so sorry, Mrs. Crispin, but I have an. . .emergency and need to speak with my fiancé."

The woman narrowed her eyes and studied Margo.

Several seconds passed.

"I'll go get him, but keep it short." The woman started to close the door.

"Please!" Margo bravely shoved her foot into the space to stop it. "It's very cold out here. Might I wait for him in the parlor?"

Mrs. Crispin let out a huff. "Fine. It's against my rules though. Your time will be shortened."

That wouldn't do. In fact, the more she thought about it, the more she realized privacy was of the essence. And she definitely didn't want to put Luke in a bad place with his landlady. Finding a good place to live was almost impossible during these times. "Never mind, ma'am. I don't want to go against your rules. That would be inconsiderate of me." She wrapped her arms around her stomach. "Could you ask Luke if he would bring a coat down for me?"

"That's a good girl. I appreciate your good sense, Miss Hunley. It's nice to see young people be honorable." The landlady closed the door when Margo moved her foot.

She turned on the porch and looked out at the gloomy night. It fit with her circumstances and made her shake even harder.

Of course, it wasn't just the chill in the air making her tremble. The note in her hand was the culprit, no doubt.

She heard the door open behind her. "Margo, are you well?" The concern in Luke's voice made her want to bury her face in his shoulder and cry. But she put on a brave face and turned around, and he held out his coat for her to put on. Pushing her arms into the sleeves, she relished the warmth of his touch to her shoulders as she wrapped the coat around her.

"No. I'm not." She pinched her lips together as tears pricked her eyes. She handed the note to him.

His brow furrowed as he took it and opened it.

He read aloud: "*Tell your boyfriend that if he knows what's good for him, he'd better quit his job and move out of town. I know what he has, and it doesn't belong to him.*"

His face paled even in the dim light of the porch. "Where did this come from?"

"It was in my mailbox." She swallowed against the lump in her throat. "What does it mean, Luke? What's going on?" Her words rushed out.

He closed his eyes for a moment, and his shoulders lifted and then sank. "Come." He took her hand and pulled her to sit with him on the steps. "There is something I need to tell you."

With another shiver, she followed him, and her heart sank. Was he in some sort of trouble?

He stared at the note for several moments and folded it up. "I was not sure how to speak to you about this. At first I was excited, but then a bit of dread followed."

"Please. . .tell me." Whatever it was, they could get past it.

He looked out across the street. "I found something while we were diving and setting the charges for the tower construction." His eyes darted back and forth, and then he leaned closer to her. "It is a large gold nugget."

She gasped. "Truly? Gold?"

"I thought it would be great for us—give us a good start to our marriage. But it began to worry me. Now I understand why. Someone did not want me to find it. I spoke to George about what I found, and he is helping me to figure out what to do."

In her mind, there wasn't a question about what to do. She grabbed both of his hands and held on as tight as she could. "It's not stolen is it?"

He shook his head as his eyes widened. "No, *mon amour*. I would never steal."

"Oh Luke, I would never think that you were capable of stealing anything. But someone is upset about it. Maybe they think that you've stolen from them."

"How can it be stealing? It does not belong to anyone. George and I both believe that there might be more down there—"

"Are you saying you want to look for more?" She pulled her hands away.

His face fell. "You do not think I should?"

Wringing her hands, she got to her feet and stood on the bottom step. "I don't know." To be honest, the note scared her.

"Margo." He reached out for her hands and pulled her down to sit next to him again. "Please. Let me go to the police with the note. But you must understand that I cannot quit my job. I made a commitment, and we need the money." His voice was strong and firm. No hesitation. "Our future is very important. This could be the answer from heaven we have been seeking. A way for us to begin our future. A way for us to bless others as well."

The thought of not having to live off potatoes and bread was appealing. What if there was a vast treasure? And they wouldn't have to worry about money ever again. They could build the big house they'd dreamed of and fill it with children and family. They could give to the poor and help the church. She closed her eyes for a moment. *Lord, show us the truth.*

But then she looked down at the note in her hands. The words made her shake again. The person—whoever they were—knew where she lived. "You'll talk to the police right away?"

A long breath came out of his mouth. "Of course. They will know what to do."

"And you said George knows?"

"Yes. He has agreed to help me."

If George was helping Luke, then it had to be all right. George had a wife and children. He wouldn't do anything reckless.

Margo laid her head on his shoulder. Everything would be all right. It had to be. "Please just promise me something."

"Anything, my love."

"Don't keep anything like this from me again. We're about to be married. We need to be honest about everything."

"I promise. I am truly sorry this has happened. We should pray about it, and I will speak to George about the note as well. Maybe the person who wrote it will come forward and we can talk to them. Perhaps then everything will be fine."

Wishful thinking, but that was one of the things she loved most about him. His optimistic attitude even in the darkest of times. "You're right. We should pray about it." She put a hand on his cheek. "I hope that your penchant for seeing the best in people is correct."

"Time's up." Mrs. Crispin's voice behind them made her sit upright.

She got to her feet. "I'd better get back home." The door clicked shut again.

Luke gazed up to her, his eyes full of sorrow. "Let me walk you."

She took his elbow as he got to his feet. "Thank you."

"Tomorrow is our special dinner?"

She nodded and gave him the best smile she could under the circumstances. "Yes, it is. You'd better not be late, Mr. Moreau."

"I would not dare even to entertain the idea."

The whole way home, she couldn't help but feel that someone was watching her. All because of that note. But Luke held tight to her hand and told stories from his childhood that made her laugh.

She loved the distraction. Hopefully the police would know exactly how to help, because she didn't want to live her life looking over her shoulder all the time.

Back at her boardinghouse, Luke stopped at the base of the steps. "Until tomorrow then." He gave a slight bow to her and kissed the back of her hand.

The gallant gesture made her shake her head. "Oh Luke. I do love you so."

"Sleep well, Margo. I love you." He waved and took long strides back up the hill.

For the moment, her heart could be content in the knowledge that Luke loved her. That he would speak to the police. That everything would be okay.

But what would tomorrow hold?

Luke
March 16, 1933

The officer behind the counter read the note and handed it back to Luke. "We've been getting a lot of reports of threatening notes, Mr.

Moreau. Most are much worse than this." He shrugged. "This one doesn't even have any specifics."

"A lot of reports? You are telling me that this happens to many others?" Relief began to trickle into his mind.

The officer made a face that Luke didn't understand. "More than we can deal with. People are desperate and will do anything to get food and shelter."

"You are not concerned?"

The man's brow furrowed. "Oh, we're plenty concerned. Crime is up all over the city. But we can't do anything about this"—he tapped the paper—"until we know it's a real threat." The man's face softened. "Look, if I were you, I wouldn't worry. You don't look like a man that has valuables and jewels falling out of his pockets. This is probably just some hooligans playing pranks. Or possibly a coworker that might be jealous." The officer eyed him. "Go home. Get some rest. But if you receive any more notes, come see me."

What the man said made sense. Maybe the writer of the note didn't actually know that Luke had found gold. Perhaps it was some sort of prank. Taking a deep breath, he nodded at the officer. "Thank you, sir."

"You're welcome."

Luke stuffed the note into the pocket of his shirt and headed out of the station. The more he thought about it, the more he agreed with the officer. There was nothing to worry about. He could go to Margo with confidence and tell her that everything would be all right.

By the end of the workday, Luke had debated every possible scenario he could think of in his mind, hoping to convince himself that they didn't need to worry about the note. Too many other things needed his attention. Especially his job. The work could be grueling.

Coming up out of the water after his fourth dive that day, Luke let the rivulets run down his suit as the swing carried him over to the landing dock. Each dive today had gotten more difficult. And not just because he'd had to do double duty since two of the divers had quit.

Every time he went down, the pressure in his chest increased. Not the kind of pressure he expected and understood from diving. But the kind that came from worrying over a problem again and again. He didn't want to let anyone down. Doing the right thing was paramount to him.

It didn't help that he'd had a sleepless night because of that note. He'd tried to push away all thought of the gold, the ship he'd seen, and the possibility of more treasure. Tried to focus on Margo and their future together.

That was everything to him. And as much as he wanted that gold—gold that could support them for the rest of their lives—he didn't want to see anything bad happen to Margo.

The more Luke thought about it, the more he stirred himself up into a tizzy. At least that's how Margo described it. His thoughts swung back and forth like a pendulum. One minute, it was a good idea to search for more of the treasure. The next minute, he wanted to be rid of it for good and run away with Margo from the threat.

As the swing carried him back to the landing dock, he looked over at his friend.

George nodded at him.

One of the crew behind Luke unhooked the air hose, and he was free to remove the heavy helmet. Stretching his neck in all directions, he tried to get his muscles to relax.

"How was the current?" His friend quirked an eyebrow.

"Violent. I will be surprised if I do not have many bruises when I get home." Shedding the heavy suit, Luke shook his head. The layers of long johns and clothing they wore under the suits helped to keep them warm, but as soon as he surfaced, he'd often break into a sweat.

George leaned in. "Two guys are missing. Nathaniel and Michael." The whispered words made Luke's skin crawl.

"Missing?" He couldn't believe it.

"Yeah. Someone went to check at the boardinghouses where they rent, and both of them were nowhere to be found. On top of that, the rooms were a mess like someone had dumped everything out onto the floor."

Luke tried to keep his breathing steady. "What do you think it means?"

"I don't rightly know. But with Jacob and Bill quitting, we're down four divers. The bosses are trying to find others who can do the job. If they can't, then that means you and me will have to carry the load for a while." He looked left and right. "Might give us more of a chance to do a little searchin' on our own, if you know what I mean."

"You think it is safe for us to do that?" After he'd told George about the note this morning and his visit to the police, he'd thought for sure that George wouldn't want any part of it.

"Desperate times, my friend. No one knows where you found it. And it's not like it's easy to get to. I think we're safe for now, but we should probably hurry."

"Do we have someone we can trust to stay at the controls at the surface and work the hoses?"

"I talked to Charlie earlier. Didn't tell him the details, but he's willing to help us out. You can tell him the whole story if you want." George shrugged.

That was good. Charlie was someone he liked and trusted. "I keep wondering if it is right for us to use the equipment. Could we be accused of stealing?"

"Mr. Walters has already left for today. All the management is reeling from the missing workers. We could dive tonight, and if you really want to ask for permission, you can do that tomorrow."

Since George was all right with it, that should make him feel better about it too. Shouldn't it? They wouldn't be putting anyone in danger.

As the sun shifted lower into the horizon, Luke checked his watch. Margo wasn't expecting him for another two hours. That would give them a small window if they snuck back out to the pier as soon as everyone left. "Tonight then?"

"Sounds like a plan. We should go talk to Charlie and fill him in, and I need to send a note to the wife and let her know I'll be a bit later than usual. That way she won't worry." George coiled the hose and stacked the other equipment. "I guess we can take our time cleaning up. That way we don't have to put it all away and then haul it back out."

"Will you go get Charlie? I would like to send a note to Margo as well." Luke watched as the dock that had been built out across the water to the south tower site emptied of all the workers. "I am relieved that you are willing to help me, George. Thank you."

"The sooner we get it over and done the better."

He'd had the very same thought. The weight of the knowledge of what lay below the water was a heavy burden. One he would be glad not to carry anymore. "I agree."

George jogged down the pier to get Charlie, and Luke looked around as the sun disappeared. What if someone was watching?

Not only could they get into trouble for using the equipment, but what if the writer of the note really *did* know about the gold?

No. The police officer didn't think there was anything to worry about.

Searching around the area, Luke saw nothing out of the ordinary. Nothing was amiss.

George and Charlie walked toward him down the long dock. A

gentle gust of wind washed over him. Everything was fine.

Perhaps tonight would change everything.

The Son

Four down. Eight to go.

He tapped a finger on the table in front of him. Looked at the plans spread out. He'd acquired a dive suit and paid a guy to operate the controls at the surface. Even promised him a lot more money after they were done. The guy was stupid enough to agree and think he'd be rich too.

But the biggest problem still remained. How to get down there without the bridge crews knowing. If he couldn't shut down the whole thing, he'd have to get creative. And risk someone seeing them. From what he could tell, it would take a lot of trips. Gold was heavy. And it would take time to dig it all out.

Dad had left him this legacy. A chance at a new life.

Time was running short. The more they blasted away the seafloor for the bridge, the bigger chance the ship would be damaged or covered up—or worse, washed away. Along with all his gold.

Eight guys were still on the payroll as divers for the bridge. But four of them were scared. If he could get them to run, he wouldn't have to kill anyone. The other four just needed more of a shove. Something he was willing to do. Because he would do whatever it took.

Maybe a few more threats would suffice. If not, he'd have to create a disaster of some sort. Something to shut it all down, get everyone running scared so no one was diving for a few days. That should give him enough time.

But if people had to die, then so be it. If Dad could do it, so could he.

The treasure was his. All of it. Retrieving it would prove that his father hadn't lied. Hadn't abandoned him.

He pulled out the small box of his father's things. Dad's last letter sat on the top, and he reread it. Many years had passed since 1894, but it didn't diminish the feelings it brought up.

Feelings of pride. Excitement.

Obsession.

A word his mother used over and over again. About his father. About him.

But she hadn't understood. Never had. Otherwise, she wouldn't have run away from his pa. A man who had poured his life into finding the treasure so he could give *them* a better life. It wasn't greed. Wasn't idiocy. It was passion. Yeah. Focus and determination.

Proven by the risks his father had been willing to take. Like what it had taken to get the diving gear, which back in the 1890s was even harder to come by. Heavier too. So what if Dad killed a man to get it? It didn't matter. Simply proved his point.

Dad had been determined to do what he set out to do. The only things he had to go on were his father's scribbled notes. But there were enough for him to be able to figure it out. There'd been no accounts of any ships named the *Lucky Martha* being found in all these years. That meant that it still had to be down there.

And since that diver had found a piece of his gold, he knew it was. He was determined to finish what his father had started. No matter what.

Like father like son.

He *would* get that treasure.

Chapter 6

Kayla
July 23, present day

The day was absolutely perfect. Puffy white clouds dotted the sky. No hint of rain or fog. Kayla breathed deep of the salty air.

Standing on the scaffolding built around the south tower for the restorations, she put her hands on the hips of her thick wet suit that was zipped up to her waist. Her short sleeve rash guard over her swim suit gave her better freedom of movement up top as she worked with the equipment.

She'd climbed up the scaffolding to get a better view of the water from above. Funny how different perspectives gave insight into what was happening below the surface.

And this water was some of the most unpredictable she'd ever worked in. Paying attention to all the computer data was crucial, but it was even more important to understand the water and keep her senses alert.

Carrie was in the boat, dropping anchor and doing last-minute checks. Steven and his guys should arrive any minute.

Kayla ran through a mental list. She'd have to give them all the basic rundown. Then they'd suit up for the fifty-seven degree water and get ready to deal with the fun tidal schedule. If they timed it just right, they could get in four or five dives today.

Hopefully Steven's guys had good endurance. Which they should. Carrie had done a lot of investigating into Mr. Michaels's company and crew, and she'd been impressed. If Kayla's assistant was impressed, that meant she was too. Carrie was skeptical about everything and also very protective of her boss. Especially after the deaths of Kayla's parents.

The wind coming toward her brought the sound of a motor to her attention. As it rounded the peninsula from the marina, Kayla watched and thought about the man it carried.

Steven Michaels was an interesting man. After she'd updated the mayor, they'd been called back to the medical examiner's office. Not only had he asked intelligent questions, but he'd thought of several things she hadn't. She liked how his mind worked. And they seemed to work well together.

Coffee had been nice. For once she'd felt at ease. She hadn't had a conversation with a man of his intellect in a long time. Their time together was refreshing.

Climbing down from the scaffolding, she let her mind wander. How long had it been since she'd gone on a date?

Too long.

Since before Mom and Dad had died—must be more than two years ago.

Since then she'd pushed and fought to find out who had hit her mother. It was that person who—in her mind—was responsible for her mother's death, her father's death, and her current "obsession," as Johnathon put it. She'd lost friends over it. Lots of them. But it hadn't mattered before.

Now the realization hurt. She had to admit how lonely she was. And she didn't like the person she'd become. Almost like it wasn't even her and she was an observer watching life happen to someone else.

Until she'd spent time with Steven. For the first time in more than a year and a half, she'd felt like herself again. Which was odd since he was a stranger. And she'd closed her world down to a very, *very* small circle.

"You okay?" Carrie's forehead was creased in that I'm-worried-about-you frown she was so good at.

"Yeah." Kayla let out a long breath and smiled.

"It's good to see you smile." Carrie passed her a tank and gear. "You might as well triple-check before they get here. I know how OCD you are about these things." She winked.

"I'm not OCD." Kayla laughed. They had the same discussion every dive. "Just very. . .focused."

"Call it what you want, but I don't think I've ever met anyone that is quite the perfectionist that you are."

"Those are two entirely different things." Something Johnathon had been hounding her about. Being a perfectionist was true. She couldn't deny it. She was good at being in charge. Organizing. Leading. It was also why she had such a difficult time letting go.

Letting it all go was what she was supposed to be doing. But so far, that had been much harder than she'd ever thought possible. Not just because she wanted closure and to know who was responsible, but because emotionally she felt like she was being stabbed in the heart. Every day she was reminded of the loss.

The discovery of the skeleton wrapped in chains hadn't helped. Obviously a murder victim, the remains brought up every feeling related to her mother's death. The why and who. Someone was guilty of murder.

The mayor wanted answers, which meant that she had to find them. But he also wanted whatever else was down there with the ship. To him, it was probably all a huge publicity stunt. Anything to show how he had uncovered a mystery, how he was the best thing San Francisco had seen in a long while. Whether revealing the lost ship was a boon to tourism or a way to refresh everyone's minds about their incredible history on the peninsula, it was still a stunt. It made her want to choke on her coffee as she took another sip.

But she was the archaeologist and the one who figured out all the answers. Even though the mayor didn't want to wait, he also wanted the story. That put her smack dab in the middle of it all.

The smooth engine of the sleek Intrepid 300 purred as Steven steered his boat next to hers. "Good morning." Danny and Tim waved at her from the seats behind Steven and another guy she hadn't met yet.

"Good morning." She grabbed the rope Steven tossed to her. "Nice ride."

"Thank you. She's a good boat." He patted the console.

It looked clean too. Obviously the man knew how to take care of his things.

As Steven's crew tied up the vessel, he jumped onto the scaffolding. "All right, Boss. We're ready."

She grinned at the nickname. Carrie often used it for her. But among these muscular surfer-dude males, it made her want to laugh at the picture. "Since the current's pattern at the moment is perfect for getting us where the *Lucky Martha* resides, I think it's best to dive from here. But when the current shifts this afternoon, we'll need to use both the boats and anchor out past the drop-off."

"Sounds like a plan." Steven's smile did things to her heart. Things she couldn't take the time to understand at the moment.

Focus. They had a big job ahead. "All your gear ready?"

"Yep. Danny double-checked everything before we took off. Tim triple-checked on the way over." Steven pushed his arms into the sleeves of his wet suit, pulled it up, and zipped. "Just give us the instructions, and we will be your extra hands."

"Perfect." Leader mode was her go-to. She just hoped they could do it the way she explained—the way *she* would do things. Because she really didn't want to have to go behind them and fix everything. In her mind, she could hear her counselor telling her to let it go. Again. *"Let go of the reins. Let go of the control. Let go of the need for everything to be perfect."* She couldn't be in ten places at once.

As she gave the guys specific directions on what they were trying to accomplish on the first dive, she couldn't help but watch their faces for any reactions that showed they didn't understand. But there were none.

She covered the specific hand signals they would need to use and described how to dig around fragile items—especially human remains. Which, at this point, she expected to find more of. But she wished they could just focus on the artifacts that were down there. Items that could help show the world what it was like in the mid-1800s aboard a vessel that wasn't owned by anyone of wealth. It was a working man's—a poor man's—ship.

What she couldn't understand was why there were bones from the different eras. If they were the same age of the ship, that would be one thing. But for all the tests to come back verifying the results that they were from the 1890s and the 1930s. . . It didn't make sense. If the boat sank in 1849, how did those two die?

In her mind, it was easier to reconcile 1930 a bit better since that was around when the bridge was built. But 1890s? And why was that person wrapped in chains and. . .murdered? Was it all about the ship? Or could it be that the tides and currents simply buried the body in the wall where the ship now lay?

Shaking her head, she focused on the guys in front of her. They had a lot to do today. Hopefully the water would cooperate.

"With the turbulence of the water, we can't use the underwater communications I like to use in calmer waters, and we probably won't have much visibility." She handed each guy a slate and wax pencil. "We'll go old school and attach these to our wrists. You'll just have to get pretty close to be able to read, and we'll keep using simple hand signals."

"Got it."

"Sounds good." The guys all nodded to everything she said, and then they shrugged on their gear, testing mouthpieces, masks, and air lines. Danny and Carrie were the ones designated to stay up top with the boats on the first dive to help if necessary, and Steven and Kayla both held buttons to call for help. The plan was to get in as many dives today as possible, and they'd brought six extra tanks per person.

They were ready to go.

After getting thumbs-up from each of the team members, she jumped in, adjusted her mask, then kicked away from the boat and went under. Turning on her props, she headed toward the coordinates she had programmed into her dive watch.

The water was intense in the strait. No matter if it was a calm day or not. Under the surface, it always seemed to be a tug-of-war of tides and currents.

Thankful for the propeller helping to pull her in the correct direction, she flicked on her light as she went deeper. The depth of 120 feet was still in the safe range, but the chill of the water could be felt through her suit. That's why each dive shouldn't be too long. No one wanted hypothermia.

She kicked herself over the underwater cliff, and for a moment the water calmed and the darkness around her seemed quiet. Still. Then her light hit the structure. It appeared as if it were literally carved into the wall of the strait, but she knew that the ship had been buried by the waters over time. The silt and mud of the strait was ever changing.

Seeing the *Lucky Martha* again was exhilarating. Even if the last time she was here she'd found a body. There was something about touching history. . .wanting to know the story behind it all that drove her on for each dive. And even though this one was ripe with legends and stories that she wasn't certain were true, she wanted to know the whole story. Longed to find out what had happened. Why the ship had sunk. What they had been carrying.

How the crewmen lived.

No matter how many incredible things she'd brought up from watery graves over the years, each one was new and different and made her excited about their history all over again.

The other guys joined her as she guided her glove-covered hands over the wall. This was a different part of the ship than where she and Steven had been before. She needed to get to that same location and see if she could find any other bones. Scooting along the edge of the ship, she searched for the spot.

The current picked up and shoved her to her right. There. A hole in the wall. That was where they'd found the skeleton. It was clear that they had disturbed this area before. Where much of the side of the ship was smoothed out by the rushing water, this area was dug out.

She motioned to Steven, and he came up beside her and nodded. He agreed it was the spot.

Letting their DPVs float by the tethers to their waists, they used their fins to kick and keep in place. Between the two of them, they worked at the same area and tried to be as gentle as they could.

Each diver had a bag attached to their waist where they could collect items that needed to go to the surface. The other guys began to work around the bow and stern as she had instructed them. A lot of work had to be done, and having all the extra hands would save her a huge amount of time. But the really delicate part she wanted to handle herself. Carrie called her a control freak, which always made Kayla laugh. Because frankly, she was. But it made her really good at her job.

After almost ten minutes of digging at the same hole, she grabbed onto something long and thin. She closed her eyes and realized, yes, it was probably another human bone and there was no need to panic. She just needed to get it out and bring it to the surface.

Handing the object to Steven, she saw it for the first time. Yep. Another bone. Which meant there were probably more to be found.

He put the bone in the bag and tightened the drawstring. Then frowned. The bubbles around him were different. More prevalent.

She watched his face as he checked his gauge and signaled to her that his air was low.

How did that happen? They had full tanks when they went down, didn't they?

The other two divers approached and signaled the same thing.

What on earth was going on?

She looked at her own gauge. She had a good twenty minutes left.

She hated wasting the dive time and debated staying by herself, but if the guys were running out of air, they all needed to resurface. It was the only way to be safe.

Giving the signal to go back up top, she slowly made the ascent and used her props to get her back to the coordinates of where they'd left the boats.

But for some reason, her skin crawled. Her heart sped up, and she felt the telltale signs of a panic attack closing in. She was responsible for all these people. What if they ran out of air before they surfaced?

Her breaths came faster and faster.

No! Stop. Calm down. Breathe. Using the square breathing technique, she forced herself to focus on the surface. Slowly. They were almost there.

As her head broke the water up top, she removed her regulator and took a big gulp of air. Then she watched as each guy made it up as well.

There. Each diver was accounted for. Alive.

But it didn't take away the awful sensation building in her gut.

Someone had messed with the tanks. Why?

Steven

Back at his office, he had the team going over every inch of the gear. It didn't make sense. Why had every single member of *his* team started to lose air? It wasn't exactly the best way to make a good impression on Kayla.

He went over each moment of the dive. Right before she'd handed him the bone, he'd noticed a few bubbles emerging and had heard a sound that reminded him of the fizz of ginger ale. That was why he'd checked his gauge when he did. All the others said the same thing. It started at different moments, but it was across the board. Every one of his team.

Thankfully, it hadn't happened to Kayla. Of course, she'd brought her own tank and gear.

What did that say about his team? He paced the room and placed his hands on his hips when he reached the window staring out at the view of the bay. Something was wrong. He wasn't sure what, but in his gut, he knew.

A knock sounded at the door. He walked over and opened it. "Kayla." Hopefully his surprise didn't show too much. "Come in. Please." It was a nice surprise. If only they didn't have to deal with the catastrophe that happened earlier. And had essentially shut down all their work for the rest of the day.

She nodded and set her backpack down in a chair.

"What can I do for you?"

"I'm just checking in on what you've found out about your tanks. I have to say. . .I was a bit worried."

He strode around his desk and sat down. "I must admit to the same. And I'm not a worrier. But nothing like that has ever happened to us."

She fidgeted with a thin gold band on her right hand. "Does

anyone know that you are helping me with the project?" Her voice cracked.

"Nope. Not a soul. Everyone knows that we were doing restoration on the tower, but nothing else." He steepled his fingers. "What are you thinking?"

"I don't know." She shook her head, and her shoulders lifted as she took a deep breath. "But something doesn't feel right. Ever since we brought up the skeleton, I haven't had the best feeling. At first I thought it had to do with. . ." She stopped herself and didn't say anything more.

"With what?"

She shook her head. "Doesn't matter. I know that's not it now. But I can't shake the feeling that someone doesn't want us down there. Like there's someone watching that shouldn't be. I have no idea why." She leaned back in the chair and crossed her legs.

"Maybe it's just because now that we know there's a mystery surrounding the ship—and not just the legend of gold—a murder mystery, you're feeling anxious because of it. I'm sure in your line of work, you don't come across a lot of that." He wasn't sure if his words would be encouraging or not. But he tried.

She let out a soft chuckle. "You'd be correct. I deal with things that have been buried for decades and hundreds of years. There's not a lot of talk of murder—just how old something is or isn't."

"Well, my guys will get to the bottom of it. I assure you."

"But what if someone is trying to. . .sabotage what we're doing? We can't take risks under the water like that. I can't be responsible for putting people's lives in danger. And when all of you were losing air today, it really made me panic. That's not a normal occurrence."

"The panicking or the loss of air?" He tilted his head and smiled.

"Both." She shook her head at his attempt at humor. "I don't like things going wrong. I'm a bit of a perfectionist and double-check, even triple-check everything. Every time. I want everyone to be safe. That's got to be my utmost priority."

"I hear you. I'm the same way." He leaned forward and put his elbows on the desk. "I'm sure we will figure this out."

"But you have to agree that it's not a coincidence?"

"Yep. Not a coincidence." He stood up and came around the desk to get right in front of her. Her face had paled, and he wanted to do anything he could to ease her stress.

"That's what I thought you would say. That means I have to ask the next question. Is there any chance that one of your guys did this?"

"No. No chance." There wasn't, but he understood that she had to ask the question. He would have done the same if he were in her shoes.

He watched her face as she processed. Her eyes seemed to look deep into him, searching for answers.

"I trust my guys implicitly." Yeah, it was hard finding guys who stayed with the job, because most of the men who were skilled and talented divers were also adventure seekers. Surfer types, yes, but they were the best. Steven had always had to be a little generous with them about time and schedules, but if he asked them to be there, they were there. They knew how to keep things confidential. They knew how to do their jobs. It simply couldn't be one of them.

"I was hoping you'd say that. But I had to ask." She looked away and flicked her long hair over her shoulder.

Right as he was bending over to scratch his calf. The ends of it hit him in the face.

"Oh, I'm so sorry. My hair has a mind of its own."

"Yeah, I have that problem too." He swiped a hand over his head.

The serious look disappeared, and she laughed.

Standing up, she moved to the window. "My dad used to tease me about how my hair could be used as a weapon."

He laughed with her, but in an instant her laugh faded. As if the memory were bittersweet.

Crossing her arms over her chest, she shook her head again and again. "I just don't get it. I don't know what to think of all this. I want to get down there again to finish the job, but now the ME has asked that we wait until he gets some results off of the bone we brought up today. It might be nothing, but I have a feeling he's got some sort of theory too."

"What did the mayor say?"

"As much as he wants to do all of this ASAP, he agreed to it. There's no need for him to worry, right?"

"I take it you didn't tell him about the loss of air?"

She turned to face him and grimaced. "No. Do you think I should have?"

He stood and took a few steps toward her so he could see her face better. "I think you did the right thing. Since we don't know who knows what and who's behind it, I think we should keep a lot of things to ourselves. I think if you can trust me and I can trust you. . .we should be good."

Her expression gave away the weight of her thoughts.

Yes, they were in a serious situation. But he wanted to take the weight off her shoulders. What he really wanted was to spend time with her. Without the stress of the project and the tanks losing air and the mysterious murder of a man from the 1890s.

"Hey. Why don't we go get some dinner. Let's not even discuss anything about diving. I think we both need to give our minds a break from all this and simply enjoy some good food. I don't know about you, but I'm starving." Hopefully he wouldn't scare her off.

Her face relaxed. "You know? That sounds really good. As long as you know a good place for seafood and steak."

"You got it. This time it will be my treat."

"I'll take you up on that." She actually looked more relaxed than he'd ever seen her as she grabbed her backpack. "I definitely need to get my mind off all of this."

He opened the door, and they walked out into the hallway. It was almost like a date. At least in his mind it was. Hey, a guy had to start somewhere.

"I need to take your team out at some point to thank them for everything."

"You might want to save up for that. My guys can eat."

She laughed. A light, beautiful laugh that made him feel warm inside. "Who says guys are the only ones with that talent?"

"Oh, do I hear a challenge?" He scanned her slim, five-foot-eight figure. "I can eat a whole pizza by myself."

"So can I." She lifted one eyebrow but kept on walking.

He couldn't help his expression.

"Don't look so shocked."

"A little thing like you?" She had to be pulling his leg.

"Longtime swimmer here. When I was at my best, I ate almost eight thousand calories a day." She winked at him as if in challenge. "And you know as well as I do that we burn a lot when we dive. Especially when we have to kick so hard just to stay in one place."

He tipped his head. "Wow. I'm impressed."

She elbowed him as they walked. "You should be." Then she rubbed her hands together. "Now let's just see if you can afford to feed me."

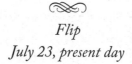

Flip
July 23, present day

He sipped his coffee as he padded barefoot through the sparse studio apartment. Living outside the city saved him some money, but not enough to afford to live in more than this little box.

Soon that would all change.

Flip sat at the bar and looked through the piles. Tidal charts, half-filled notebooks, receipts from the coffee shop.

Ah. There it was. The journal from good old Augustus De Ville. It was chock-full of details. To think that the ship had been found *twice* and the gold never retrieved. He let a grin slide onto his face. Too bad the guy died before he could do anything about it. Seemed Augustus and his daddy had nothing but bad luck.

On the other hand, he'd had the good fortune to find it. He'd almost thrown out the old book as junk. But he hadn't. Because he was smart and had good instincts. Now the gold was his for the taking. As long as he could delay Kayla Richardson and Steven Michaels. But that was trickier than he'd thought. Still, the holes in the air hoses had been a good start.

Taking another chug of coffee, he opened the journal. Back in 1933 they didn't have the technology and dive equipment that he had today. Augustus's loss was his gain.

His iPhone dinged, and he checked the screen and smiled as he picked it up. Perfect. His friend in the coroner's office had succeeded. The dirt he had on the medical examiner helped Flip secure more time via a neat little bribe.

Setting his phone back down on the counter, he took another long swig of coffee, draining the cup. Shouldn't take too long before he had everything he wanted. His wife had called him a loser. But he'd prove her wrong soon enough. Then she'd be back. And they'd get back to where they were before everything fell apart. She wouldn't have to work so much—or at all if she didn't want to—and would realize he was worth having around. Just because he was a little laid back and enjoyed an adventure every now and then didn't mean he was lazy. He could make a fortune and still do what he loved. And he'd have her. Forever. He'd never let her leave again. Never.

Flipping through the journal, he tried to see if there was

anything important that he'd missed. Any clue that could help him. But thanks to the restoration team, he now knew exactly where the *Lucky Martha* lay. Coordinates couldn't shift either, because it was firmly buried in the seawall.

The only thing that stood in his way was Kayla and her stupid job for the mayor. If he could just keep them from the job for about a week, he'd be able to get everything he needed.

What a wonder to live in the age of technology. The mayor hired an archaeologist for the history. Probably wanted to make a big story of it and line his own pockets. But Flip would yank the rug out from under them. He had all the history he needed.

Augustus's father, Leo, had searched for the treasure in the strait for years. But no sooner than he found it, he'd died. Thrown from his horse. Pitiful.

Then Augustus had taken up the mantle when he'd gotten older. From the sounds of the journal, all he cared about was proving that his dad hadn't been a lowlife and hadn't just abandoned them. While Leo De Ville was most definitely a lowlife, Flip felt a connection with the man. He wanted to prove himself to his wife and child too. Just like him. The difference was, Flip wasn't a loser. He wasn't a lowlife. He deserved that treasure. Deserved to have his wife and family back.

Pretty soon he'd be having the Hollywood elite over for dinner parties and showing off his mansion and cars. No one would belittle him for catching a few waves. No one would call him lazy.

Amazing what a little money could do.

If he had to get rid of a few obstacles in his way, then so be it. It was his turn to call the shots.

Chapter 7

Margo
March 16, 1933

She lit two candles on her tiny table and then checked everything. Smoothing her red skirt, she smiled. Wouldn't Luke be surprised? She actually had a small roast, potatoes, carrots, onions, and bread to feed him. It would be a feast compared to what they normally ate. She'd have to eat bread the rest of the week and next without anything on it or to accompany it, but the sacrifice would be worth it.

A knock at the door made her heart jump. He was here!

She went and opened the door.

"For you, my love. I am sorry it is later than we planned, but thank you for waiting for me." He held out a single rose. Something he'd probably spent a pretty penny on—just for her.

"Oh my goodness." She put a hand to her chest. "It's beautiful. Thank you. I will wait for you. . .always." With her other hand, she took the flower.

"Ah, *mon amour*, it thrills my heart to hear it." He kissed her on the cheek. "The rose is not as beautiful as you, but I wanted to do something special." Taking her hands in his, he dipped his head. "Before we speak of anything else, I must tell you that I spoke with the police this morning about the note."

She'd done everything in her power to push that subject to the back of her mind, hoping and praying that Luke could take care of it and it would all go away. "And? What did they say?"

"There is a lot of crime now. People desperate. They do not think that we have anything to worry about. It could simply be a prank."

"Do you feel that is true? That it's just a coincidence? A prank?" How she wanted to believe it was true.

Luke took a moment to think. Another thing she loved about him. Rarely did he jump to conclusions or speak hastily. One of the many reasons why she trusted him with her whole heart. "I believe it is. I cannot imagine that anyone could know about the gold I found. I was underwater and have not shared it with anyone other than you and George. Since the police officer was not concerned, I do not believe that we should be either." He held up a finger. "But he did say that if we receive any other notes or threats, I should bring them to him immediately. Just to be careful. I want to tell you everything. But I do not think we have any reason to worry."

The depth of sincerity in his eyes was enough to convince her. "If you don't think we should worry, then I won't worry." She lifted her lips in a smile. "Thank you for going to them. It gives me great peace of mind."

He placed his hands behind his back and lifted his nose in the air. "Now, before my stomach turns itself inside out, I must ask. . .what is that delicious aroma?"

His words made her blush and broaden her grin. "It's a roast of beef."

His eyes widened. "My mouth is watering already. I haven't had beef in a very long time."

She shut the door behind him and pointed to the table. "You don't have to wait any longer. Please, have a seat." The thrill of being able to feed him something so special put an extra spring in her step. It was wonderful to be able to take care of someone she loved so very much.

As she sliced the meat and put it on the two plates, she let her thoughts drift forward. Is this what it would be like to have money? To be able to feed her husband and family with plenty of food? Food that tasted good. What it would be like to be able to prepare grand desserts and baked goods to present to friends and neighbors as gifts. The thought was almost too much to take in. They'd lived in poverty for so long—the Depression had been so very difficult. Could there actually be a light at the end of this long tunnel?

"Oh Margo, it all smells so tantalizing." His deep laughter made her look up. "Did I use that word correctly?"

She giggled at how he looked like a young child squirming in his seat. "Yes, you did. Have you been searching the dictionary again for new words?"

"Oui." He shrugged. "I am proud to be an American now."

She spooned gravy over the top of the meat and potatoes, then sliced her loaf of homemade bread. "There's not any butter, but hopefully it will be good enough with the gravy." Carrying the two plates to the table, she smiled and took a deep breath. She wanted to savor this moment for a long time.

When she placed the plate in front of him, he closed his eyes and inhaled. "Let us pray and thank the Lord above for this bountiful table."

As she took her seat, he held out his hand. Taking it in hers, she squeezed it and closed her eyes.

"Father in heaven, we thank You for the blessings you have bestowed on us. The food before us that Margo has so delicately prepared is a gift from You, and we thank You for it. Thank You for giving us to each other. And for the jobs that You have provided. We want to offer up our thanks for everything to You, for You are almighty God. Just as You provided manna for Your people in the wilderness, You have provided beef for us in this time of great hardship. Help us to savor every bite and to be thankful for whatever we have to eat each and every day. Help us to give to others and to show Your love to those around us. And if it be Your will, Father, give us direction on what we should do about the gold. It is in Your precious and holy Son's name that we ask all these things, Amen."

"Amen." She placed her napkin in her lap and gazed at the man she loved. There were moments that took her breath away. This reminder of his deep faith was truly her favorite thing about him. What a godly husband and wonderful father he would be.

He lifted a forkful of beef and gravy to his mouth. "What are you staring at?" He grinned as he shoved it in his mouth.

"You."

"Mm, well you need to eat, my love. Because you are entirely too thin as it is."

"Oh hush." She shook her head. While the difficult times had made it easier to lose the bit of weight she'd carried on her hips, she hadn't starved herself and still considered herself heavier than most of her friends.

"It is true. You need meat on your bones. At least, I believe that is the words they use?"

It made her laugh. "It amazes me how you remember so many of the new phrases you learn. I have a tough time simply learning a few words in French, and yet you learn more and more each day."

"I love it that you wish to learn my language. I will do better at taking the time to teach you." He closed his eyes again and groaned. "This is the best meal I have ever eaten. I wish for you to enjoy it as well."

She grinned at him. "Thank you, Luke. Although I'm sure you've had much tastier fare, I appreciate the compliment." Her stomach growled as the scent overwhelmed her taste buds and made them water. She scooped a forkful of the beef and gravy up to her lips. As she tasted it, she let out a little sigh. It did indeed seem like the best meal ever—probably because they knew to appreciate it all the more.

He wiggled his eyebrows at her. "It is delicious, is it not?" He sopped up gravy with his bread.

"Goodness, I'd almost forgotten how wonderful beef tasted." Trying to tell herself to slow down, she really had to work at it, because she wanted nothing more than to scrape her plate as quickly as she could. The rich gravy tasted heavenly on her tongue.

"How was your day today, my love?" He took a sip of water and smiled at her, his eyes twinkling in the candlelight.

Lifting her napkin to her lips, she smiled back. "The children were quite rambunctious today. They miss seeing their parents, and I can see that it is taking a toll on them."

"The parents are working extra hours?"

"Yes, pretty much as many as they can get. She goes in early in the morning, and he stays late at night. They each get about an hour with the children. But I don't think they get to see each other very often." How lonely that must be.

That couldn't happen to her and Luke, could it?

"It must be very hard trying to keep their family spirits up when they have to focus on just keeping food on the table."

"You've hit the nail on the proverbial head, Luke. Another fun English phrase for you to add to your vast vocabulary." Margo let out a sigh and put down her fork for a moment. "I am worried about them. They don't have faith like we do and seem to be short with one another all the time. At least from what I see. The spark of love isn't there, and that saddens me."

He reached across the table and took her hand. "Let us make a promise to one another at this moment that we will seek to keep God first, our marriage relationship next, then our children and family— all of those above the priority of job or money or anything else."

With a quick dip of her chin, she squeezed his hand again. "I promise, Luke."

"Margo, I promise it to you as well. With God as my witness, I will keep my word."

Her heart soared as he leaned across the table and laid a gentle kiss on her lips. As long as they kept God first, the rest would fall into place.

Lying in bed that night, Margo couldn't fall asleep. Tossing and turning, she shoved her pillow back under her head and let out a long sigh. Dinner had gone so beautifully, she hadn't wanted it to end. They talked about all their dreams. Their hopes. And then Luke had told her he wanted to show her something and pulled out the gold nugget. It had taken her breath away. To think that there could be more gold under the waters of the strait. That gold could be the answer to all of their financial woes.

Luke and George had gone down again to the ship and dug through mud and silt the waters had layered upon the outside of the vessel for all these years. His excitement was clear. Both men were convinced they would find more.

Which could be just a dream. But at least it gave them some hope for right now. They probably didn't have a lot of time to try and gather it anyway.

Her thoughts turned to the note. If the police weren't concerned, then she shouldn't be either. Maybe it was a coincidence. Or maybe the writer of the letter had put the note in the wrong box.

Maybe they didn't have anything to worry about after all.

But even as she told herself that, her heart caught in her throat. Were they doing the right thing?

Luke
March 20, 1933

The day couldn't have gone better. After days of doing an extra dive each night and trying to dig around the ship to find access, they'd finally uncovered a hole in the side. He and George had found two more nuggets. Two! George kept one and Luke kept the other. Now the only problem was that they were scheduled to set off charges each day this week. Their boss wanted to finish clearing as much of the seafloor as possible to try and catch up since they were down on men.

The ship could be damaged in the process—or even moved. Then they might not be able to find it again.

Coming up out of the water for the sixth time that day, Luke decided that they needed to talk to their boss. It was the only way to continue. Besides, he was tired of the secret. It felt wrong to use the equipment without permission.

Once he and George were back at the locker room, he grabbed his things and checked to make sure no one else was around. Then he went to his friend. "I think we need to go speak with Mr. Walters."

"You're worried about the charges, aren't you?" George sat on a bench and shook his head.

"Yes. I am. Aren't you?"

His friend nodded. "What do you want to tell him?"

"I am not sure. Let me pray about it as we walk over there. I just know for certain that we are supposed to speak to him about this."

"Lead the way. You're the one who found the first nugget and the ship. I'll be there for you, but don't expect me to say nothin'."

It didn't take long for them to make their way over to the office. The door was open and Mr. Walters spotted them. "Come on in." He waved them in. "Please tell me you're not here to quit. I need some good news."

"Oh no, sir. I love my job. George does too. We have no wish to quit." Luke held his hat between his hands.

"Good. You two are my best divers, and we need you." The boss looked down at all the papers on his desk. "And we are incredibly behind schedule."

"We will work hard for you, Mr. Walters." Luke looked at

George and then back to their boss. "Speaking of the schedule, sir. . .that is actually why we came to speak with you." *Lord, give me the words to say.* He bit his lip, took a deep breath, and plunged ahead. "The current hit me pretty hard on one dive and knocked me over the edge and up against the seawall."

"You all right, Moreau? You weren't injured were you?" The man looked up over the rim of his glasses.

"No, sir. I am quite well." Another shaky breath. "But what I found is what has me concerned."

"Oh?" Their boss looked back and forth between them.

"It's a ship, sir."

"Oh, there's lots of ships that were sunk during the gold rush." This time he looked at him full on. "I forget you may not know the history, Moreau. But half the city was built on top of ships that were scuttled for their lumber. Men came from all over all in their search for gold. Many of them abandoned their ships. Why, there are even sunken ships all along the coast that were used as landfill to expand the shoreline." The man waved a hand in the air as if to dismiss them.

"But we believe this ship has significant value." How much should he say? "That is why we would like to request that the charges be delayed for a few days. And we ask for your permission to use the dive equipment to search the ship."

That got his attention. Mr. Walters put his hands on his hips and stared them down. Then he took off his glasses and swiped a hand down his face. "Boys. I can't believe you would ask that when you know good and well how far behind we are."

"I mean no disrespect, sir." Hopefully he hadn't just put their jobs in danger.

"Look. I know you two. You're hardworking. And I greatly appreciate the fact that you asked permission to use the equipment. But there is no way that I can delay the charges any more. I wouldn't have thought you two to be treasure hunters, but hey, everyone needs hope every now and then." He rapped his desk with his knuckles. "Since you're my best guys and I need you. . .I will give you permission to use any of the equipment that you like in your off time. . .if you'll give me an extra hour in the mornings. Deal?"

"I can do that. What about you, George?"

"Yep." His friend nodded.

"The charges will *not* be delayed. Understood?" Walters put his glasses back on his face and looked down at the desk again.

"Understood, sir. Thank you, sir." Luke turned on his heel and gave a wide-eyed look to George. They rushed out of the room together and headed straight back to the locker room.

"Did he really just give us permission to use the equipment?" George's face showed his intense shock. "I wouldn't have believed it if I hadn't heard it with my own ears."

"Yes, he did. But that means we do not have much time."

"Then I think we need to go down again tonight."

"Are you most certain? What about your family? I have kept you and Charlie late for several days now."

George shrugged. "My wife knows what's going on. Besides, it won't be for very long. We only have a couple of days before we might not have any more chances. Charlie said he can do it every night too."

Excitement rippled through him. Now that they had found more gold, he understood why people got gold rush fever. He couldn't help but smile. "Then let us go down."

"I'm afraid the tides won't be in our favor tonight, so it will be much harder."

"We can manage. We always do." Luke quickly changed into his diving gear. Tonight could change their lives.

Three hours later, they returned to the locker room with more energy than they'd started the day with. Luke couldn't stop smiling.

And as he looked at his friend, the same appeared true for him.

"I can't believe we found more gold." George whispered the words to him and then looked around. No one was out and about at this late hour.

"It is a blessing from God above." Luke felt the gold he'd placed in his pockets.

George slapped his back. "You keep on prayin', my friend. Because it seems that God has His ear bent to you." His friend was the best of the best. Honorable. Trustworthy. Supportive. Luke was thankful he could share these blessings with him.

Luke reached over to his friend and put his hands on his shoulders. "I pray that the treasure we found will bless your family for many years."

"Thank you." His friend shoved stuff into his locker as he grabbed his other things. "I hate to be in such a hurry, but I can't wait to share this with my wife." The smile that stretched across his weary face was the biggest Luke had seen in a long time.

"Go. I will finish cleaning up and lock the door. You have missed too much time with your family already."

George nodded at him and ran out the door.

Luke took his time making sure the space was clean and ready for the next day. It felt good to relish the thought of all they had accomplished. They'd even made the hole large enough for them to fit through. There was much of the ship to be explored. But after the charges were blown, it could be gone. He would have to be content with whatever the outcome. He had done the best he could.

After he locked the door and headed out, he shoved his hands in his pockets and looked out at the water. Amazing that so much lurked beneath the lapping of the waves. He'd never been one for ghost stories or legends. But he understood now how men got caught up in the hunt for gold and treasure.

Tomorrow couldn't come soon enough. Because that might be

all the time they had.

Shaking the thoughts from his head, he looked toward the heavens. "Lord, forgive my attitude. If this is all the time we have, then help us to be grateful for it and the blessings You bestow on us. Whatever may come, I will trust in You."

As he looked back to the water, a glimmer caught his eye. What was that? He stepped closer and squinted. The metal swing was creaking. He heard it. There. And there again. There weren't any boats out in that area.

Light from the moon glinted off something again. Something small.

He blinked several times and tried to focus. A shadowy figure took shape.

Was someone else out on the water? Diving?

No. He must be seeing things. No one could dive alone.

Chapter 8

Kayla
July 23, present day

Their server brought her another plate of shrimp and retrieved the plate full of shells.

"Thank you." She sent him a smile and then looked at Steven.

"I have to admit, when you said you could eat, I didn't believe you." He laughed as he cut into his steak. "I thought I was the only one with that talent."

"And what do you think now?" This was the most fun she'd had in a long time. It was so comfortable to be herself. No one to impress. No one to try and prove herself to.

He chewed his bite and winked at her. "I am not about to get myself in trouble with the lovely lady for remarking on her eating habits." Taking a swig of his tea, he smirked. "But I will say I'm impressed."

"It's mutual." She pointed her fork toward him. "I've never seen anyone put away an appetizer platter, a salad, that huge bowl of San Francisco cioppino, and what was that? A sixteen-ounce steak? Plus a baked potato."

"Don't forget the broccoli. I have to eat my veggies, you know."

The look on his face made her laugh out loud. Oh, it felt good to laugh. Really laugh. "Forgive me for not mentioning the broccoli. I'm sure you'll probably order dessert as well?"

"Of course! I hear they have some of the best crème brûlée in the city."

She moaned. "Oh, that is my favorite."

"Then you'd better save some room." He lifted his steak knife and went back to work on the massive piece of meat. After he had sliced the rest of it into pieces, he lifted his fork again. "The first time I was living on my own, I called my mom and dad after I had to buy my own groceries and apologized."

"Why is that?"

"Because I realized how much I had cost them over the years."

How thoughtful that he had even thought about that. The layers to the man in front of her ran deep. "You know, my mom used to always talk about how much time she spent cooking and how many times a day she ran the dishwasher, and I guess I just didn't think anything of it. But now that you mention it, if I think back, when she said she had to run it three or four times a day, it makes me realize how much I ate and how many dishes I used." She lifted her shoulders and sent him a grin. "Between early morning workouts, two-a-days, and everything else, I did probably eat six or seven times a day. I was a swimmer and a growing teenager—I guess I thought that was normal." Her heart twinged a bit. If only she'd thought of it before now and thanked Mom for all she did over the years. Now it was too late. She took another sip of water and tried to push back the thoughts. She didn't want to ruin this nice evening with her grief and guilt.

He leaned forward and put his forearms on the table. "One time I was over at a friend's house for dinner, and his mom made homemade lasagna. I didn't know what to do when she only put one pan out on the table."

The look on his face almost made her choke on her water. "Let me guess, you ate half the pan?"

He shook his head. "My mom always made two pans. One for me and one for the rest of the family."

"So what did you do?" She couldn't keep from smiling. His face

110—KIMBERLEY WOODHOUSE

was priceless as she imagined the teen version of Steven struggling with the situation, trying to have good manners.

"I took the serving that she gave me and tried to eat as slowly as I could. But I still finished before anyone else. Went to bed hungry."

"You poor thing. I bet you wasted away."

"Almost. I ate breakfast at their house and then ran home. Mom made me another half dozen eggs."

She shook her head and kept her mouth closed as she laughed. His deep chuckle filled the aching hole in her heart. Good food. Good conversation. The night out was exactly what she needed.

"Tell me, Miss Richardson, what is it that you like to do in your free time?"

The question caught her off guard and the horseradish in the cocktail sauce made her cough. After a sip of water, she patted her lips with her napkin. "Promise you won't laugh?"

"Now, why would a gentleman laugh?"

"Because my answer might surprise you."

He set his utensils down and leaned back. "I'm hoping it does. You surprise me at every turn."

"Oh?" She narrowed her eyes at him. "All right. Challenge accepted. I like to crochet."

"Now see. I did *not* expect that. What have you made?"

She shrugged. "Blankets, baby booties, hats, a few sweaters— pretty much anything and everything I could get a pattern for. I'm a history fanatic, so I watch documentaries and crochet."

"Do you think you could make me a sweater with long enough sleeves?" He stuck out his arms to his sides and knocked a glass of water off a server's tray. "Oh, I'm so sorry!" He jumped up and helped the girl clean it up.

The server blushed and told him everything was fine—it happened all the time.

Kayla had her napkin over her mouth and silently laughed until tears streamed down her cheeks.

"See the problem?" Steven grinned and sat back down. "I'm six foot four and can't find shirts or sweaters to fit my arms for anything."

Regaining her composure took a few moments. When she did, she lowered her napkin and attempted to keep a straight face. "I could definitely give it my best effort, but you might go broke buying enough yarn."

It was his turn to laugh. They continued to eat, and when their server came back, they ordered dessert. As their dinner plates were cleared away, Steven leaned forward again and rested his arms on the table. "I noticed that you've lived in San Francisco for quite a while. What do you like most about the city?"

"The weather." She didn't even hesitate. "All until Indian summer in September. I'm not a fan of the intense heat. The rest of the year is just perfect."

"Even the fog?" He tilted his head.

"Yep. Even the fog. I love how it rolls over the water." She leaned forward as well and fiddled with the saltshaker. "What about you?"

"The burritos." He nodded emphatically.

She shook her head. "I should have known that it would entail food."

"Yep. But I'm sure you know what I'm talking about. Burritos, street tacos. . . Man, I get hungry just thinking about them. Best I've ever had."

The man had just put away ten pounds of food, and he was talking about being hungry. She couldn't stop laughing. Tears burned her eyes, and she started to wheeze because she couldn't catch her breath.

He held out a hand. "I'm sorry. I'll behave myself."

Putting her napkin to her eyes again, she waved him off. "No. It's totally fine. I enjoy laughing."

With a chuckle, he reached for his coffee cup. "I guess I'm just shocked that you think I'm funny. Usually my dad is the only one who laughs at my sense of humor." He sipped on the brew as the server delivered their desserts.

Crème brûlée in little heart-shaped dishes. The sugar on top was caramelized perfectly. Not burnt. No grains of sugar left. It was gorgeous. As she dipped her spoon into it, the custard held as she crunched through the topping. Not runny. Not stiff as a board.

Again, perfect.

Then she tasted it. The vanilla bean had obviously been soaked in the cream. The flavor was outstanding. "Yum." More words weren't necessary.

"I second that."

They ate their dessert in relative silence, each enjoying and savoring the bites with a comment here and there about how full they were but how the crème brûlée hit the spot.

Steven finished his in about four spoonfuls. As he licked the utensil, he lifted his eyebrows at her. "So. . .since I'm newer here, I have to admit that I've never driven down Lombard. Would you care to take a drive with me down the 'crookedest street'?"

Polishing off her crème brûlée, she nodded and set down the spoon. "I would love to. But if you want to drive down the crookedest street, we'll have to hit Vermont Street in Potrero Hill."

"Really? I thought Lombard held the title."

"Why don't we go see for ourselves? Rest assured, while many people still think of Lombard as the 'crookedest street in the world,' Vermont actually holds the title for its sinuosity."

"Sinuosity? That's a new one." He wiped his mouth with his napkin.

She pointed to his smartphone sitting on the table. "Look it up. You'll see what I'm talking about."

With a sly glance, he picked up his phone and typed on it with his thumbs. "Ah, I see now. Apparently a Travel Channel show even did an episode on which one was more crooked."

Kayla took another sip of water. "Maybe I should drive."

"Why?"

"Because you probably aren't used to driving your big SUV around tight curves like that, whereas my Bug is a pro at it."

He laughed at that. "I will gladly try to squeeze myself into your little bitty car if you think it will be more fun." The sparkle in his eyes made her feel warm and fuzzy inside.

"It'll be worth it." With a lift of her eyebrows, she grinned. "We'll be able to go faster too."

He patted his stomach. "Maybe we should let our food settle a bit." He winced.

"You're so funny. You're probably ready for your next meal already."

"Like a hobbit. Second breakfast, elevensies, luncheon, after-noon tea, dinner, supper—yep, that about sums it up."

Once again, the guy impressed her. She leaned back and crossed her legs. "Are you a Lord of the Rings fan, or have you just heard that reference to your eating one too many times?"

"Big fan."

"Me too!"

"I—" His phone rang, and he checked the screen. "Excuse me, but that's one of my guys. Let me make sure that everything is all right."

"Of course."

He answered his phone, and his brow crinkled as he listened. "Are you sure?" He shook his head and paused. "Thanks for calling. I'll call the police in the morning, and then we'll have to check all the other gear and replace all the hoses. Just in case." Tapping the red phone icon, he ended the call and looked up at her. "Looks like we have a problem."

"Oh?" Her stomach dropped. It must be about the loss of air in the tanks.

"Each hose had a man-made hole in it. Appeared that they filled it with something that dissolved over time in the water, and then the leaks began. It wasn't an accident or a coincidence. It was intentional." The weight of the admission lowered his shoulders.

"What do you think it means?"

"I have to admit that I hoped there could be some weird explanation for it. But now the only conclusion I can come to is that someone didn't want us down there very long. If they wanted to get rid of us, they could have done a number of different things. This. . .well, this seems more like a threat. But why?"

The hair on the back of her neck tingled. "The *Lucky Martha*. That's why."

Steven

The parking lot was full as they walked out to their vehicles. The evening with Kayla had been the best one he'd had in a long time. Maybe ever. And he didn't want it to end now.

Spinning his keys around his fingers, he broke the silence. "Look, I know the call from Tim was a bit of a downer, but let's not let it ruin the evening. We could take that drive."

She stared at the ground for a moment and looked up at him. The serious expression in her eyes began to fade. "You're right. Let's do it."

"You still willing to chauffeur?"

She looked him up and down. "Sure. But your first inclination was correct. You might not fit."

After squeezing himself into what he deemed her little kiddie car, she put the top back down and drove through the city. The first several minutes were eerily silent.

"Well, there's still an elephant in the room—er, car—isn't there?" She raised an eyebrow at him.

"Yeah, I guess no matter what, it's still there. But we don't have to focus on it. Why don't we agree to put it on the back burner until tomorrow morning?"

"You sure you'll be able to do that?" Her focus was on the road, and her hair whipped out behind her.

"No. Not really. But I'll try if you can."

"Deal." She sent him a small smile and then looked back at the road. "All right. Let's do Lombard first."

"Perfect." They were at the top of a hill, and Steven saw the first curve in the brick road ahead. With cement walls, shrubs, or high curbs on both sides of the street, he cringed. "I'm glad I didn't bring my truck. I don't think I would have fit."

She waited at the top for a minute. "It's definitely tight."

He watched the lights of the car in front of them as it wove back and forth down the hill.

"Ready?" She grinned.

"Ready." He gripped the arm rest in the door just to be dramatic.

Her laugh washed over them as she drove down crooked Lombard Street.

But when they made it to Vermont Street, he cringed. "I don't like not being able to see what's coming next."

"I know. It's a bit disconcerting. Especially in the dark with all the trees."

As she maneuvered around the curves, her hair flew in his face several times.

"Sorry!" But she kept her eyes on the road.

Wiping at where it had tickled his face, he blinked several times. "I didn't realize there was so much of it. And how heavy it is."

"Like I said, it has a mind of its own."

Thirty minutes later, Steven let out a long breath as he unlocked the door to his home. Exhaustion seeped into every cell of his body. But he couldn't help but smile as thoughts of a blond-haired under-water archaeologist took center stage.

His phone buzzed with a text.

Everything locked up. Sorry about the news.

Great. The reminder of the reason for Tim's phone call burst the nice train of thought. Nothing like that had ever happened to him, and it was still a bit of a shock.

It was confirmed that someone had sabotaged the hoses. Pretty cleverly too, since everything checked out in their pre-dive tests.

As suspected, some sort of dissolvable polymer had sealed the tiny holes in the hoses until the salt water ate through it. But would the police be able to find out who had done it and why? Their equipment was always locked up, and no one had access to it except his team. Those guys wouldn't do anything like this. He trusted them.

So that brought him right back around to where he started.

Kayla had been convinced that the sabotage had to do with the ship. But only his team's equipment had been tampered with. Not Kayla's. It might have nothing to do with the *Lucky Martha*. Which made him feel better about her safety. But that meant someone might have a quarrel with *him*. Or with his company. Possibly one of his guys.

He prided himself on outstanding work. His company had a stellar reputation. Five-star reviews across the board. Everything he did, he wanted to be honorable and trustworthy. He didn't cut corners. His whole life he'd wanted to impact the world for good. So how on earth had this happened? Why was someone targeting them?

Maybe it had something to do with the restoration of the bridge. No. That was unlikely.

That brought him back to thoughts of the ship. If someone

knew about it and wanted the chance to retrieve any treasure for themselves, that could be motive.

The whole thing made him uncomfortable. The mayor's office probably had a good five or ten people who knew about what was going on. One of them could easily have slipped information. But who would be bold enough—and ingenious enough—to sabotage the air lines? The act obviously wasn't meant to kill any of them—but most definitely to scare them.

Sitting on his couch, he propped up his feet.

His phone rang, interrupting his thoughts, and he answered. "Hello?"

"Hey, Steven. This is Kayla."

Just the sound of her voice made him sit upright and smile. "Hi."

"I just got off the phone with the mayor and told him about what happened and what your guys discovered. I also told him you would be calling the police in the morning to investigate, but he insisted that he should be the one to do that since we are working for him. He wants to keep it under wraps and out of the press, so he's calling the sheriff himself."

Of course he was. The mayor was a control freak. And a good one at that. "All right. I'm not as worried about the vandalism to the equipment as I am about the motivation behind it and everyone's safety."

"Me too." She yawned. "Sorry. I had just begun to think about getting some sleep, but the mayor wants the sheriff to meet with us tonight at your offices. I know that makes for a very late night for you after I had you in the water so early. I'm sorry."

Even though his body was weary, the thought of seeing her again buoyed his spirits. "It's not your fault. I'll do whatever is necessary."

"Can you round up all of your team to meet us there?"

"I'll do my best."

"Should we say half an hour?"

"Sure. Not positive I can get all the guys there by then, but I'll be there."

"See you soon." She hung up, and his phone beeped that the call was disconnected.

He leaned back for a moment and ran a hand down his face. Who knew how extensive the sheriff's investigation would be tonight? Long night indeed. But if it helped them get answers, that was worth it. That was what they sorely needed. Especially before they did another dive.

Dozens of questions plagued him. But he pushed them all aside, stood up, and went to splash water on his face. Might as well freshen up while he was at it.

Back at his offices for the fourth time that day, Steven unlocked the main entrance and flipped on all the lights. He walked down the hallway to the equipment lockup and checked the door. It was secure.

That made the question of who was behind it even more prevalent in his mind. If someone had broken in, the alarm system would have notified them.

He shook his head to clear it of the thoughts and went back out front to be ready for all the arrivals.

Kayla and the sheriff entered at the same time. The sheriff had two men with him.

"Thank you for coming, sir." Steven held out a hand, and the sheriff shook it.

"Sorry it's under these circumstances, but we will get to the bottom of this." The man commanded attention and exuded authority. He turned and spoke to his men in hushed tones. Looking back to Steven, he raised his eyebrows. "We need to see your equipment."

"Of course. Follow me." Steven led them all down the hallway to the secured room. Keying in the code to the lock, he then put his thumb on the screen to be scanned.

"That's a state-of-the-art system you have there." The sheriff and his men put gloves on. "How many people have the code and can gain entry?"

"Only my crew. They are all on their way here now."

The officer nodded and grunted. "Good. We'll need to talk to each of them separately. It happened this morning?"

"Yes." Steven turned the lights on in the equipment locker. "The guys discovered tonight what had happened and called me. That was when I told Kayla that I would be calling the police in the morning to investigate."

He turned to Kayla. "You don't have access to the equipment?"

"No, sir. I have my own team and equipment." Her voice sounded tight and weary.

"It wasn't tampered with?"

"No."

The sheriff grunted again.

What was he thinking?

Steven watched Kayla's face. She narrowed her gaze. "Is there anything I can do to help?"

"Not at the moment. I understand that you are in charge of the project and the mayor asked you to be here, but it's going to be a long night, Miss Richardson. I apologize for that, but we will need you to stay along with all of Mr. Michaels' men."

Chapter 9

Margo
March 22, 1933

The past two days had been glorious. Luke had been on cloud nine as he told her about what they'd found. They sat on a bench at the park and dreamed about all the things they could do with the gold. Even made a list of all the people they wanted to help first. Then they wouldn't need to wait to get married or build a house or have children. She could even stop working soon. As much as they loved San Francisco, they'd even talked about moving somewhere else. Or traveling. The sky was the limit.

Her heart soared as she thought about the man she was going to marry.

Luke was good. Strong. Loving. Cared about other people. Their life together would be wonderful.

Staring out across the Pacific Ocean as her little charges played in the sand at Ocean Beach by Golden Gate Park, she couldn't imagine a better life ahead of her.

Pulling her sketch pad out of her bag, she looked back at several of her drawings from the past few days. Some of them were dreams of the future, some were more like a journal. She flipped to a clean page and began to draw the children as they used their little buckets to try and build a castle.

The water was much too cold for them to be able to play in it right now, but they loved the sand, and she didn't mind cleaning up the mess from it when they could enjoy the sunshine and laughter. She'd have sand in her stockings forever, but she didn't care.

"Lookie, Miss Margo!" Little Maria pointed to the tower of sand she'd sculpted.

Even though it resembled the Leaning Tower of Pisa, it miraculously didn't fall over. With fast fingers, Margo went to capturing the moment on paper. Little girl with pigtails. A boy dumping his bucket of sand over his legs. Both all smiles. Sand towers covering the shore around them.

The sun warmed her face as they approached the noon hour. She'd probably freckle even more, but she didn't care. There was something so positively glorious about sitting on a white sandy beach, the sun kissing her skin, and the laughter of children floating around her.

A perfect day.

If only Luke were here.

As she finished the sketch of the children, she turned to another sketch. One she'd been working on for weeks.

Luke.

She'd tried to capture the blue of his eyes, but something about it made it feel like it wasn't quite there yet. Tilting her head, she examined the sketch and questioned what it was that seemed to elude her in the drawing. Maybe it was simply that she couldn't put on paper how his eyes twinkled. How the edges of his eyes crinkled when he smiled and laughed.

Then it hit her. What it was really lacking was depth.

It was one thing to see Luke's face on paper. But that was flat.

And there was so much more to him than what she could sketch.

Looking back up at the children, she tapped her pencil against the paper and thought about all the things that made Luke who he was.

Inspired anew, she began to make a list on the side of the portrait. Maybe she'd be able to draw him more accurately with the list right there in front of her.

"Miss Margo! Miss Margo!" Little Bobby waved his hands in the air. "Look at what I did!"

His chubby cheeks were pink as his face filled with a proud smile. He'd managed to bury himself up to the waist in the sand.

Margo laughed and waved back. "That is quite impressive, Bobby. What are you going to do next?"

"Eat lunch!" He clapped his hands together.

"You want me to bring your lunch to you now?"

His head bobbed up and down.

While there wasn't a lot of food to spare, Margo had taken to giving some of her own bread to the children. They were growing and always seemed to be hungry. She couldn't bear the thought of them not having enough.

As she brought the brown bag over to them, she wished she had some fruit or cheese to share with them. When she was a child, they'd picnicked at the beach a lot. And oh, what fun they'd shared! Her favorite part had been when Mama brought out the picnic basket and spread out the checkered cloth. Fruit, cheese, bread, pickles, little cakes. Back then that had been simple fare, but it sounded like a feast to her now.

Would the country ever get past these dark times?

It didn't seem like there was a lot of hope for that anytime soon. The world had been plummeted into the Depression.

Maybe she should ask Luke to share a bit of the gold with this family. They had been so good to her, giving her a job, taking care of her when she needed it most. She'd love to give more back to them and to the children. Especially if it would help feed the family and take some of the pressure off of both the parents. Watching them be worn down a bit more each day was so hard.

As the kids munched on their peanut butter sandwiches, she gave them each a quarter of her own. The sun always seemed to give them more of an appetite.

The waves crashed along the shore, and the sound soothed her. The blue of the sky blended with the deeper blue of the ocean at the horizon, where she couldn't tell where the water stopped and the sky began. She could stay here forever. Where all her cares seemed to disappear. Everything seemed clean and perfect and fresh.

A sticky hand patted her face. "Miss Margo. . .whatcha thinkin'?"

She scooped the little girl up into her arms. "I'm thinking about how much fun it is to tickle you."

Maria squealed as Bobby wiggled his legs and burst out of the sand to join in the foray.

Giggles filled the air as she tickled the children and they tried to tickle her back. Then they started a rousing game of tag on the sandy beach.

When she was out of breath and laughing so hard she could hardly see, Margo plopped onto the sand and the kids raced to her open arms.

What joy it was to feel their sweet little arms go around her neck. What would it be like to have children of her own? The thought made her heart swell. Luke would be an incredible father. She could picture him tossing their children up in the air and catching them. Holding them in his lap as he read to them out of his French Bible. Holding their hands as they walked along the beach.

Bobby began to droop in her arms. Nap time was upon them, and she needed to get back to the house and check the laundry she'd hung out on the line earlier. "Let's go, my sweets. Can you each carry your shovel and pail?"

Maria nodded, and her curls bobbed up and down, but Bobby whimpered and snuggled up closer to her.

"All right. Looks like I might need you to carry your little brother's pail too. Can you handle that?"

"I'm a big girl." Maria picked up the other pail and stacked it with hers. Her little hand reached up and grabbed Margo's. A yawn stretched across her face.

Margo laughed. "Sounds like we *all* might need a nap." They walked over to her blanket where her bag and sketchbook lay. "Let me set you down for just a minute, little one." She laid Bobby down on the sand while she stuffed everything back in her bag. But when she closed her sketchbook, a piece of paper flew out.

Maria chased it for a few steps and brought it to her.

With a glance at the paper, Margo's heart dropped.

I warned you. Tell your boyfriend that if he doesn't listen, he won't have a pretty girlfriend anymore.

Luke

Running a hand through his hair that desperately needed a haircut, Luke yawned. He couldn't get the image he'd thought he'd seen that night out of his mind. If the shadowy figure was someone actually diving, did that mean someone was after his treasure?

It had kept him up entirely too late the past two nights.

Maybe it was time to stop digging around that sunken ship and just focus on his job. It might even be good to find another job. If he could. Getting away from the temptation couldn't be a bad thing. But where would he find another job? They weren't exactly plentiful right now. If a man had a job, he stuck with it and thanked the good Lord that he had one.

As he walked to work, he tried to shift his thoughts. Lack of sleep made a man do all kinds of strange things.

The morning dives were spent setting charges. After lunch today, they would be blowing the whole line. Whether they'd still be able to find the ship after that was the question that he and George had asked each other a hundred times. The bell rang for lunch, and they all traipsed to the makeshift dining hall.

George sat in the lunchroom across from Luke. Neither of them said a word for the first ten minutes as they ate and shared a questioning glance every now and then.

His friend had been elated to find the amount of gold that he had, and he talked about starting fresh somewhere else. His wife wasn't particularly fond of the city and wanted to have a farm out in the country. Luke had shared the dream of building Margo the house they'd talked about. But there'd always been a bit of gloom that hung over both of them after they shared their excitement. As if something bad was about to happen.

Yesterday one of the new guys had talked about the curse that was over the ships that lay in the strait. That if anyone dared disturb their resting places and dig for treasure, they would bring the curse down on everyone around them.

The man had been a natural storyteller and held the attention of a roomful of workers with his dramatic voice and big, fancy words. But at the end of the day, it had just been a story. Luke should be thankful for what he had and leave it at that. The stress of all the extra dives and worrying about curses, notes, and someone else after the treasure was enough to drive him mad.

He had to make all of it stop. The Lord had blessed him with so much, it was time to think of his future with Margo and focus on what God wanted him to do next. As he watched his friend, he realized that George didn't look like he was getting a lot of sleep either. "How are your children doing, George?" A safe and happy topic.

"Lucy has another ear infection." The man shook his head. "It's the third one this year, and we're beginning to worry. But the doctor says that there's not a thing we can do about them. Just let her grow out of it."

"Does it cause her a lot of pain?"

"You see these bloodshot eyes?" George pointed to his face. "These are the eyes of a father with a screaming child who can't go to sleep."

"I am very sorry about that." He grimaced.

George chuckled and tapped the table. "It is worth every minute, my friend. And when it is your turn to become a papa, I will be there to encourage you through it."

They shared a smile as the bell rang for them to go back to work. Luke took his tray back to the kitchen and dropped it in the bin. "Thank you!" He called through the small opening. No matter what happened, he tried to thank the people every day. And every time, he always received big smiles and waves.

He joined George on the walk back out to their dock. But men were shouting and running in every direction. What was going on?

Their boss, Mr. Walters, strode toward them, his face ashen. "We've got a disaster on our hands, boys."

"What's happened?" George stepped forward.

"Equipment has been destroyed—ropes, pulleys, winches, the motors—and *all* of the dive suits and hoses have been sliced in multiple areas. Not one of them is intact. We won't be able to dive until all of it is replaced, and we don't know how long that is going to take. This is a nightmare." The man looked out at the water. "We're already behind schedule."

Luke felt the weight of it as the truth sank in. "But sir, what about the charges? The currents will wash them away if we do not get down there, will they not?"

Mr. Walters shook his head and looked at them. "We're going to have to blow them as they are so we don't risk that."

George ran a hand down his face. "But the ocean will no doubt dump even more silt over the site by the time we get new suits.

We'll have to redo that entire stretch."

"There's not anything we can do about that. We have no way to get anyone down there, and we can't take the chance that the charges get caught up in the tidal currents and become unstable and blow. We don't know what kind of damage could be done to ships or buildings or people." He ran his hand over his beard. "Like I said. It's a nightmare."

Luke put a hand on his boss's shoulder. "What can we do, sir? Let us at least help clean up the mess."

Mr. Walters looked out at the equipment, back to them, then back to the equipment. "You're right. Let's tackle one problem at a time and focus on getting the mess cleaned up."

With firm steps, they headed down to the area where all the trouble seemed to be. How had no one seen what had happened here?

It wasn't a coincidence. Someone knew their schedule. Knew when all the men would go inside for lunch. They'd taken advantage of the moment and destroyed hundreds of thousands of dollars of equipment. How would they get the bridge built now?

The afternoon passed in grueling work, hauling dented and bashed equipment back to the main warehouse on the shore. Men in several boats were trying to salvage pieces that were still visible above the surface of the water.

So many questions went through Luke's mind. How did someone do this? It couldn't have been just one person. It also had to be someone who was knowledgeable about the machinery—and knew just how to incapacitate the bridge-building team. What if it was someone they worked with?

What if it had something to do with the note Margo found? The men who quit? The ones who were missing? Could it all be connected?

He shook his head free of the thoughts. No. His imagination

was running wild because of lack of sleep. Lots of vandalism reports had been heard around the country because people were desperate. They needed jobs. And when they were refused or let go, they turned violent in their desperation.

A cool breeze fanned his face and made him realize how much he'd been sweating. His throat was parched, and he licked his lips. Probably needed water. And food. He swiped his handkerchief over his neck and went back to the men who were trying to reconnect one of the diving swings. Without it, they couldn't lower any of the men into the water or bring them back up. Just one more thing added to the long list of devastation today.

As the sun slipped lower on the horizon, Luke's arms and legs ached. The bell rang, and the foremen shouted orders to all the men to head home before it got dark. They'd already stayed a couple of hours past quitting time.

The men were hushed as they made their way back to clock out. Everyone must be too weary even to carry on conversations. Besides, they all knew what they were facing. More work. That was a good thing when a man needed employment—but losing ground was hard to swallow.

When he reached the office and stood in line to clock out, a flash of red caught his eye. Margo.

"I'll clock out for ya. Go." George gave him a little shove.

Just the sight of her made everything inside him feel better. But as he got closer, the smile slipped from his face. She looked upset.

Wringing a hankie in her hands, tears made tracks down her cheeks.

He hurried to her and took her in his arms. "What is wrong, my love?"

Her chin quivered as she held out a piece of paper. "This."

Reading the paper, he held his breath. *No.*

"I'm scared, Luke. Maybe we need to leave."

The Son

The fog proved to be a perfect cover. No one would see them.

Larry shivered on the small dock. "How long do you think it's going to take?"

"Don't know. You just make sure that the air keeps flowing, and if you feel me tug on the rope three times, that means I need help. But I will tug ten times to tell you to start pulling me back in."

"All right." The man he'd hired wrapped his coat around himself a bit tighter. "Just hurry. It's awfully cold tonight. I don't like the fog when I can't see nothin'."

"You're not getting paid to be afraid of the fog. If you're cold, you should have brought a blanket." Some people were just downright stupid.

His helmet clicked into place, and Larry latched him in then connected the air hose. With a thumbs-up, his hired man started the air.

Because he didn't have the luxury of a swing to lower him in, he had to get creative about going into the water, but he wasn't going to let that stand in his way. Once he was under the water, the weight of the suit helped him to sink down into the dark ocean.

Funny how quiet everything was under the sea. The lamp on his helmet didn't give him much light, and for a moment, as the dark closed in, he wanted nothing more than to swim to the surface. As a kid, he'd been afraid of the dark. But then he took it out on the other kids by teasing them.

He got picked on for not having a daddy. So he picked back. It was survival of the fittest. At least that's what some dumb science teacher said.

As he sank lower into the ocean, he watched the gauge on his suit. Pretty soon he should be at the right depth. All he had to do was find the ship and he'd see how much gold was down there. Since no one else could dive for a while and he had the only working dive suit, he figured he should have at least a week to get his treasure. That should be plenty.

Without thinking it through too much, at least he'd remembered to tie a burlap sack to his waist. That way he would have something to haul up his treasure in.

The only problem would be whether he could actually trust Larry to watch the loot while he went back down, or would he need to take it someplace safe and then come back? Sure would waste a lot of time. But maybe that was what he'd have to do. He couldn't risk Larry running off with all the gold.

The gauge on his suit showed that he was at the correct depth. But he couldn't see a thing in front of him. The water looked to be thick like hot chocolate with only a little fish flitting in front of his face every now and then. Getting as close to the seawall as he could, he felt his way back and forth. The ship had to be here somewhere. But all he felt was rock and mud.

Maybe he shouldn't have come the night after they blew the charges. Perhaps it took a long time for everything to settle. Then there was the chance that the explosions had covered up the ship. Or even destroyed it. The thought made his anger burn. In that case, the gold could be anywhere. Most likely at the bottom of the strait. The gold was probably heavy enough not to be taken out on the tidal currents, unless it was small nuggets.

Going back and forth along the seawall, he found nothing. Absolutely nothing. What had happened? He knew those divers had found it. Knew they had some of his gold. So why couldn't he find it?

A tug on the rope told him that thirty minutes had passed. That meant he had only a little bit of time left. What a waste. He should have found the gold tonight. Needed to find it. But no matter how much he searched, it wasn't there.

Finally, he tugged on the rope, signaling Larry to pull him up. He kicked his legs to help Larry out and realized he needed a different plan. Maybe he'd been going about this all wrong. All he had to do was nab the divers who'd found it. Then he could threaten them and make them take him down to where the gold was. Only problem was. . .he had only one functioning dive suit.

He wanted to punch something. Hard.

There had to be another way.

Chapter 10

Kayla
July 24, present day

Miss Richardson, thank you for meeting me on such short notice."

"Not a problem, Mr. Mayor. I'm happy to help." She sat down in front of his desk. The room screamed of high-end everything. Sleek. Modern. Not a piece out of place.

"I wanted to let you know what the sheriff and his men found out."

She glanced at her watch. "So soon? I'm guessing they didn't sleep last night." It was one thing to be called into the mayor's office at eight o'clock in the morning after you'd been with the police until one o'clock the night before. But to already have answers?

"The only fingerprints on the hoses were those of Steven's team. Each of them was questioned separately, and they each had an alibi. Whoever did it covered their tracks pretty well."

Her defenses went up. She'd only known Steven a few days, but she knew for certain that he didn't have anything to do with it. "Alibis? You think that one of them did it?"

"Of course not. Mr. Michaels' team is impeccable. That's why I hired them."

Calming down, she leaned back and crossed her legs. "Do you want us to halt the dives until they can investigate further?" That's what she would do. No one wanted a saboteur out to get them.

He frowned at her. "No. That will not be necessary. I've got other plans."

"Oh?" What did the man have up his sleeve now?

"The sheriff has assigned men around the entire south tower area. On land. And on the water. They will patrol and make sure that no one is there who shouldn't be there. There is also a guard posted for your office and for Mr. Michaels'. We can't have anyone vandalizing your equipment or delaying the project any further." He clasped his hands on his desk and leaned forward. "Believe me, I am taking this very seriously."

"That seems like a lot of manpower and hours. I don't want to waste the city's resources, sir. Maybe we should just wait until the culprits can be found."

"Nonsense. Everything can move ahead as planned." He waved her off as if she were a child.

Something about the whole situation made her uncomfortable. But since she couldn't put her finger on it, she had to agree to his terms. He was the boss, and she'd been hired to do a job. She'd never quit a job before. She wasn't about to start now. "All right. Well, I guess if you don't need anything else from me, I should head back to my office and get coordinated with Mr. Michaels on the next step."

The mayor stood and held up one finger. "One more thing before you go." He leaned over the phone on his desk, pressed a button, and spoke into the speaker, "Melanie, please bring in the box for Miss Richardson."

"Yes, sir." The voice came back through the phone.

He walked around his desk. "There are some things that I am hoping will help you put together the mystery of the ship and perhaps even help solve the murder."

A beautiful redhead in a pencil skirt and white blouse carried a box into the room. Placing it on the chair next to Kayla, she smiled and walked right back out, pulling the door closed behind her.

Curiosity piqued, Kayla looked at the ordinary banker's box. "Is this it?"

"Yes." The mayor came around his desk and leaned back up against it. "You see, during the building of the bridge, the men had lockers in a warehouse where they ate and prepared for the work of the day. The crew had some troubles."

"Troubles?"

"Vandalism. . .men missing. Several divers quit."

"That doesn't sound all that unusual."

He raised his eyebrows at her. "It was when jobs were scarce and the Depression was at its height."

"Oh."

"In that box, you'll find some things that were left behind by some of the workers. I'm hoping you can piece together a little bit more of the puzzle that surrounds this. Especially since we now have bones from someone during the era of the building of the bridge. Of course it could just be a coincidence, but I'm not a fan of coincidences."

"I see." This job got stranger by the day. First it was about a treasure. A ship from the gold rush. Then a murdered man from the 1890s. Then the remains of someone from the 1930s. How did it all fit together? Trying to wrap her brain around it when she hadn't had enough sleep was proving difficult. And why the mayor of San Francisco was so interested was truly beyond her. Unless it indeed all had to do with some elaborate publicity stunt. Now *that* she wouldn't put past him. If there was one thing she'd learned about politicians over the years, it was that they loved well-placed publicity, cameras, and whatever else put them front and center.

"Let me know if you need anything. I will eagerly await your first report."

She was in the middle of lifting the box when his words sunk in. "Report?"

"Yes, in the agreement you signed. I asked for a weekly report."

Great. More paperwork. Just what she loved doing. Give her a dive suit and a place to dig any day of the week. But writing reports? Ugh. "It will be short and sweet, I'm sure, sir."

The mayor's phone rang. "I have a call coming in from the governor. Good to see you, Kayla." And just like that, she was dismissed.

"You too." The words were mumbled as she walked out of his office.

Why exactly had she taken this job? The question plagued her all the way out to her car.

She dumped the box into the passenger seat and put on her sunglasses. At this point, the only good thing that had come out of the job was getting to meet Steven.

Just the thought of him made her smile.

Well at least he could help her make it through. Maybe she should ask if he was any good at writing reports. The thought made her giggle as she pulled out of the parking garage. In fact, why didn't she call him now?

He might be interested in going through the box with her and might have some good insight.

Decision made, she told Siri to dial Steven's number. Wind in her hair, she waited for him to answer.

"Hello?" His voice was husky in the morning.

She liked it.

Maybe the day wouldn't be so bad after all.

Steven

Pressing the buzzer for Kayla's apartment, Steven ran his other hand over his smooth head. There were days he missed having a full head of hair. But most of the time, he kept it shaved because it made diving that much easier.

Her voice came through the box. "Come on up." The buzzer indicated he could come through the door, and all of a sudden his nerves kicked into high gear. As soon as she'd called, his heart had picked up its pace. There was something about her that just. . .clicked for him.

Taking the stairs two at a time, he told himself to slow down. Didn't want to look too eager. Besides, there was so much that he didn't know about her. But as soon as she'd asked for his help, he knew he couldn't refuse. If he could spend every waking minute getting to know her, he would.

And that scared him. Because no woman had ever interested him like that. Ever.

He hadn't even talked to his dad about her yet. Simply because the whole thing made him nervous.

What was different about her? Even as much as he'd thought about it, he couldn't narrow it down to just one thing. It was a hundred thousand little things.

At her door, he tapped lightly.

It swung open, and she smiled up at him. Her hair was in a loose braid swung over her right shoulder. Wearing a blue sweater over a pair of skinny jeans, she looked relaxed and comfortable. "Come in. But take off your shoes, please."

"Sure." Most of his friends had the same rule. He wasn't sure if it was a San Francisco thing or what. He left his running shoes under the bench by the door and laughed at the sight.

"What?" She turned back toward him with a puzzled look on her face.

"My monstrosities next to your little shoes." He loved the sparkle in her blue eyes. "You have baby feet." He pointed down at her bare feet.

Painted a deep shade of teal, her toenails stood out against the white carpet. She wiggled them and put her hands on her hips. "I don't have baby feet."

"I bet they're half the size of mine."

She looked at his and then hers and then shrugged. "Probably."

"See? Baby feet. They're cute." He followed her down the hallway until it opened up into a bright, cozy space. The wall of windows in front of him held the most spectacular view of the water. The room was decorated in whites and the same color as her toes.

"Can I get you some coffee? I know I need another cup after our late night yesterday." She made a silly face. "Espresso? Or French press?"

"You're speaking my love language. Espresso, please."

Her light laugh filled the kitchen as she started the espresso machine. "I have a friend whose dad always said their love language was sarcasm. He made me laugh every time. But I've never heard that coffee could be one too." Picking up a towel-covered plate, she offered it to him and removed the towel. "Cinnamon rolls, straight from the oven. You can have the whole plate." She winked and lifted a glass measuring cup full of something thick and white. "How much icing would you like on top?"

The scent of cinnamon and sugar wafted up to his nose. "Cover 'em up." For the first time in his life, he didn't feel awkward talking about food or how much he ate. It was almost like he was. . .at home.

Once the coffee was brewed and she'd added cream and sugar, she carried two cups over to the couch. "This"—she tipped her head toward the box on the coffee table—"was why I called you here."

His mouth full of cinnamon roll that was the best he'd ever eaten, he watched as she set down his cup and lifted the lid off the box.

"And the mayor said that it's all stuff from guys who worked on building the bridge?"

"Yep." Her lips formed a thin line. "Apparently this is from the guys who went missing."

"Wait. You didn't tell me that. Missing?"

"I know. Weird, right?" She took a sip and set her cup down on a coaster. "Several divers quit, then several went missing. It's so strange. And then he reminded me that this was during the Depression and jobs were scarce. It's not like guys just up and left good, steady jobs."

"So why did they leave?" Now he was really intrigued.

"That is what we are about to find out. At least I hope so."

He got down on his knees next to her in front of the coffee table. On the top sat a bunch of newspaper clippings. Not about the bridge being completed. But of when they started it. "Here, let me put all these in order by date while you see what else we've got here." Setting the yellowed and fragile papers aside, he watched as she pulled out several stacks of letters tied with string. The names on each stack were different.

A leather-bound book was next, but when she opened it up, she frowned. "Huh. This appears to be in. . ." She paused and studied it for a moment. "Maybe it's French?"

He leaned in closer and looked over her shoulder. "Yep. Definitely French. But very neat handwriting."

"That's what I was thinking." She laid the book down beside the stacks of letters. "It makes me wonder how we lost the art of beautiful handwriting over the years. I definitely wish mine was better." She pulled a rolled-up paper out of the box. "But my Grandpa's? His handwriting looked like John Hancock's."

"What's that?" He watched as she unrolled the paper.

"Oh my goodness, it's a copy of the plans for the bridge." The paper was brittle and yellowed. "Here, help me hold it up."

Steven took one end of it, and she took the other. "These are hand drawn."

"No printers or copy machines back then." Kayla studied the plans. "It's magnificent. Now *this*—this is why I do what I do."

"I can see why. It's pretty thrilling to see an artifact like this." Something in the box caught his eye. "Look. I think there's some photographs in there."

"Let's lay this down on the dining-room table." She dragged him along with her—the document between them as she took four glasses out of the cabinet—and they made it to the table, where she placed each glass on one corner of the plans. "Hopefully that won't damage it too much. I want to see how much of the drawing can be saved. But I'm afraid the paper is pretty delicate." Turning on the balls of her feet, she headed back to the box.

This time she sat on the couch, and he dared to sit as close as possible so they could look at the contents together.

"You were right." Lifting out a stack of photos, she went through them one by one. "I should put on some gloves, but I think I left them all at the office. Remind me to wipe them down when we're done to get the oils from our hands off them."

"Okay." He leaned closer and looked at the past coming alive in front of them. "Look—can you imagine wearing all that to dive in? The metal helmet alone probably weighed forty pounds."

"I can't even. . ." She shook her head. "That would be hard to trust. Knowing that your air came from someone up at the surface. What if a whale came by and dislodged your hose? Or you got caught on something? What those men must have endured to build the south tower is astonishing."

"I wonder who all of these people were? And what's the significance?" He couldn't help it—he was caught up in the mystery as well. "These are obviously from some kind of celebration. Look at how many people were gathered. But there's no bridge in the background."

"That must be from before they started construction." Her face was so close that her breath fanned his cheek. "I wonder what happened to the men who had these things in their lockers. Or if there are any clues in here to what happened. It definitely doesn't talk about any missing divers in the history of our city. The bridge was a huge feat and was celebrated for years."

"Maybe I could brush up on my French." He picked up the journal, flipped through the pages, and winced. No. Three years of French in high school weren't enough. "I take that back. We should get a translator to work on this right away."

She set down the photos and picked up the last of the papers in the box. "Wow. This is a telegram. From the president of the United States."

"Really? Which one?" History of the presidents was one of his favorite topics.

"Hoover." She pursed her lips and peered up at the ceiling. "I think I remember reading somewhere that there was a big parade and groundbreaking ceremony that generated more public interest than anything since the opening of the Panama Canal. I bet this telegram was read at the ceremony."

Steven picked up the stack of newspaper articles. "I bet it might be in here somewhere." Taking great care not to damage each thin sheet of paper, he found one dated February 26, 1933. "Here. But look, there's something handwritten around the edge. . . . I can't quite make it out."

She scooted even closer and stared at it. "It is pretty faded. I think this word right here is. . .*engaged?*"

"I think you might be right. Wait. . ." He picked up the journal again. "The handwriting. It matches, doesn't it?"

Flip

He steered the boat around the horn to find two police patrol boats by the south tower of the bridge. What? Why were they here?

The blare of a horn drifted over the water, followed by a voice through a megaphone. "This area is restricted. Please return to your harbor."

He brought the throttle down and let it idle. What to do now?

"This area is restricted." One of the police boats sped toward him. When it was within about ten yards, the man with the megaphone lowered it, and they let the boat drift closer. "No diving allowed, sir. You need to turn around and go back."

"Has something happened?" Maybe if he acted like the innocent tourist, he could gain some information.

"Just restoration on the south tower. What's your business here?"

"Whales." It was the first thing to come to mind. "I study them underwater."

"Well, you'll have to go elsewhere. I doubt they'd be in the strait now anyway with all the work that's being done." The officer's stern face told him more than the pat little story they were telling.

He leaned and looked around the police boat. "I don't see any work being done."

The officer glanced over his shoulder. "It's underwater."

He held out his hands, palms up. "Officer. . .please. My data isn't complete, and I won't be able to finish my dissertation without a few more dives. I've already paid a pretty penny to rent the equipment and this boat. Isn't there any chance you could make an exception? For science?"

"Sorry, son. No. You'll have to finish your research elsewhere." He pointed, "Now head on back before I'm forced to ticket you."

His temper flared, but he kept his mouth shut. If it wouldn't cause such a ruckus, he'd pull out his gun and shoot the stern look off of the officer's face.

Chapter 11

Luke
March 25, 1933

The repair work down at the bridge was depressing. Every time they fixed one thing, they found another problem. Whoever had done this knew what they were doing. And they'd created a lot of chaos.

The only thing he had to look forward to was a picnic with Margo tomorrow. He told her he would plan the whole thing and take care of the details so they could have a long chat. She was stressed—the second note had really gotten to her. As it should have. But he couldn't quit his job. Not now. They needed the money.

Money.

The gold that he had hidden in his room was plenty of money. But for some reason, he didn't feel like it was his. At least not yet. Maybe he was feeling guilty.

"Moreau!" The foreman hollered at him. "We need you over here!"

His thoughts went back to the job at hand. Something wasn't right here either. After all the devastation and vandalism, he'd begun to think that it was somehow connected to the ship. The treasure. The notes to Margo.

Men had quit their jobs. Others had disappeared. Why had they left? Had others come upon the ship too? Had the mysterious note writer sent threats to other divers?

It didn't make sense.

None of it.

Morale was down with the crews too. Some were talking about a curse. Others said they would do their jobs and that was it. They didn't want to risk their lives or families.

Was he wrong not to take the first note seriously? The police officer had shown more concern when he'd seen the second note. But they still couldn't do anything about it. That didn't make Margo happy, and it made Luke feel like a failure.

The thought of something happening to Margo made his heart ache. She was everything to him. His whole future.

A little nudge in his heart made him wonder if he'd been greedy. Maybe they *should* leave.

Lord, I just want to provide for my family. What should I do?

Sunday after church, the sky was cloudy, but the sun seemed to be trying to peek through every chance it got. Luke carried the picnic basket and blanket out to a grassy section of the park. He wanted everything to be perfect. After a long time of prayer that felt like a tug-of-war with God, he was convinced that he hadn't done anything wrong.

Now he just needed to make it all up to Margo. Assure her that he could keep her safe. And he would work as hard as he could to provide for her. They were going to make it.

He had a plan. It would work. It had to.

Margo walked across the grass toward him, and her lips turned upward slightly when she saw what he'd prepared. Looking over her shoulder, she seemed uneasy though.

He took her hands and kissed her cheek. "I missed you."

"You saw me at church not more than an hour ago." Her brow

furrowed. Normally she would tease and banter with him. But a cloud hung over them.

"Nevertheless, I missed you." He pointed to the blanket. "Please. Have a seat. Let me serve you today."

Her mouth tipped up again—ever so slightly—but the smile never reached her eyes.

He poured a glass of lemonade and handed it to her.

"Thank you." Her words were hushed. Resigned. After she took a long sip, she shook her head. "I'm sorry, Luke. But I'm afraid I can't do this."

"Cannot do what?" He knelt in front of her.

She stared at him for several seconds and lowered her head. Moments of silence passed, and he watched as she brushed a tear away.

"My love, I have a plan. I was hoping to feed you and show you a lovely picnic that would take your thoughts to a happy place. But let me just explain. I think we should get married. Right away. That way you can quit your job. You can live with me. I can protect you. Take care of you. Everything will be okay."

Her head stayed down. "You want to stay here?"

"Yes. I have a good job. Then there's the gold—"

"No." She held up a hand and lifted her chin. Tears filled her eyes and spilled down her cheeks. She blinked several times. "I think we need to leave. I couldn't live with myself if something happened to you or to the children I care for. . .all because of some silly treasure. Money is what we all work for. Every day. As if it's the savior of the world. The thing that keeps the world spinning. I know that. I feel that in my bones every single day as I scrimp and save enough to have bread to eat. I'm tired of the same old dresses that I've been wearing for years. My shoes are wearing thin. Just like you, I was caught up in the gold and the thought of never having to worry about money again. . .but not anymore. Don't you see?"

Her voice pleaded with him. "Someone evil seeks to harm us—all because of money." She swallowed and lifted her chin even higher. "I've made a decision. I want to move away."

"Away? To where?"

"My mother's cousin is my only living relative. He's in Michigan and works on the Great Lakes. He said he can get you a job. We could get married tomorrow—or even today—and just leave. Start fresh." For the first time that day, he saw hope in her eyes. "We have enough gold to provide for a long time. We don't need to hoard it. Please."

He sat back on his heels as his heart sank. She really wanted to move away. But all their dreams had been to stay right here. Build a house. Raise a family. He brushed the thoughts aside. "Is this what you truly want?"

She let out a heavy sigh. "Yes. I can't live with this threat over me. I'm scared for myself. Scared for you. Scared about everything all the time."

He nodded. "All right. If this is what you want. But I cannot leave right away. That would be dishonorable to my employer. They are already without several employees. I will put my notice in first thing in the morning and stay until they find a replacement."

Margo's shoulders slumped a bit. "How long do you think that will take?"

"A few weeks, perhaps?"

With a turn of her head, she looked out to the east. She didn't say anything for several minutes. "All right." Her tone was hushed. "But I still think we should get married right away. I need to quit my job. I can't put the children or their family in danger. Just know that I won't stay here forever, Luke. I won't be able to sleep if I'm living in fear."

"Oh Margo. . .I love you so. I will protect you. I promise."

She burst into tears and flung herself into his arms. "I'm going to hold you to that promise."

Margo

That night in bed, Margo cried for hours. She would finally be getting married to the man she loved.

But the circumstances were less than ideal. They weren't anything like the dream that she'd always had. They'd asked their pastor if he would marry them, and he agreed for tomorrow evening. It was hard not to have any family to share in it with her. How she missed her parents. But she wouldn't wish them back to this world of suffering for anything.

To make up for the lack of family, she'd had dreams of her perfect wedding day. But it wasn't to be.

She had no lovely dress. No flowers. Nothing.

There would be no party with their friends. No scrumptious cake.

And she was okay with that. She really was. But it didn't take away the sadness over the loss. And it definitely didn't take away the fear.

The threatening notes had been taunting her ever since she arrived back in her room. How many times had she read them and tried to figure out who would do such a thing? How did they know who she was and where she lived and worked? They lay on the table in the room, mocking her.

Throwing her covers aside, she made up her mind. She would burn them. That's what she would do. It wouldn't get rid of the threat completely, but she should have done that already. Tomorrow was a fresh start. And soon they wouldn't be here anymore.

They would go somewhere far away where they couldn't be found.

Luke had promised to protect her. He was a good man. The

gold had distracted him, but he was still a very good man.

She'd spoken with her landlady and said she'd move everything out the next day. But the family she worked for asked if she would finish out the week. Mrs. Albright's mother was coming to live with them sometime in the coming week because she was couldn't pay her rent and had no place to go. Once she arrived, the children could stay with their grandmother during the day, which would save the family money. Margo was relieved that she wasn't leaving them in the lurch, and it confirmed in her heart that she was doing the right thing. If only Luke hadn't hesitated and wanted to stay longer.

He was doing the right thing though. In her heart she knew that. He was an honorable man.

A shiver raced up her spine.

But the fact remained that two men had disappeared. And two others had quit. Why? Had they been threatened too? Did that mean that she and Luke—and George and his family—were in even greater danger?

Jobs weren't something that you thumbed your nose at during this economic crisis. What would make men just up and leave them? The more she thought about it, the more afraid she became.

Her grandmother's words from when she was a child echoed in her mind: *"Fear is not of the Lord, child. He is almighty God and has His angels watching over you. So there's nothing to fear."* Every time she'd had a nightmare, her grandmother would pray over her and say those same words. Every. Single. Time.

And Margo had always calmed down.

After the notes were reduced to ashes, she climbed back in bed and pulled the covers up around her ears. Staring at the ceiling, she felt the puffiness in her eyes from all the tears she'd shed. Her throat was raw. As a child, her faith had been stronger.

What had happened to her? Why was she doubting?

Closing her eyes, she poured out her heart to the Lord. The words gushed forth, and she confessed her sin, her anger, her fear. *Father, forgive me for my lack of faith. Help me to rely on You. Please take away this fear and doubt and show Luke and me what path we need to take next. Help me to rest in You, oh Lord my God.*

Her heart felt lighter, but the pressure in her head remained. Too little sleep and too many tears.

She just needed rest. Tomorrow would be her wedding day. Then she and Luke would be together forever.

They would only be here a few weeks. They could make it that long. She could stay hidden in his room and make sure he had food to eat and a warm bed to come home to.

Then they would go to Michigan. A new life awaited. And all the threats and talk of treasure would be a distant memory. One that could easily be forgotten.

Chapter 12

Steven
July 27, present day

In the chilly water of the Golden Gate Strait, Steven, Tim, and Danny assisted Kayla and Carrie as they carefully dug around and uncovered artifacts from the *Lucky Martha*. More than 170 years of mud and silt from the turbulent tidal currents had made the sea's topography around her ever-changing. It was a wonder the ship was still there and not carried out in chunks deep into the Pacific.

No more delays. No more waiting. The mayor was after them to get as much done as they could as quickly as possible.

In the first dive of the day, they'd dug through a wall of mud that had been at least two feet thick, but it had paid off. Not only had they found the skull and multiple bones that must belong to the tibia that the ME still had, but they'd made it through to an open area.

With a narrow opening wide enough for them to swim through, they had gained access to the interior of the ship.

Now, on their second dive of the day, with fresh tanks and bags for artifacts secured to each of their suits, they were ready to see what Kayla wanted to examine first.

Steven had to admit that he understood why she had gone into the field of underwater archaeology. When they'd pored over that box from the 1930s, he'd been transported to a different time and place, and it fascinated him. History had always been one of his favorite subjects, but it took on a whole new meaning when you got to have your hands on things from real people from almost a century ago.

If his company wasn't so good at restoration, he'd consider doing archaeology himself. Especially if that meant he could work with Kayla Richardson on a regular basis.

A signal from her brought his thoughts back to the present. They were ready to go back into the ship. She led the way, and he followed. Up top, she'd given each of the guys a specific job, detailing what she was hoping to find. If things worked the way she hoped, they would be streamlined to accomplish it.

With small hand tools, she deftly worked around what appeared to be a wooden door. Like a trap door in the floor of a deck. Her hope was that it was one of the ship's holds. She described it like a smuggler's hold. One that was below the others and unknown except to the crew in case they were attacked by pirates.

It made perfect sense that she would be correct, because when they'd made their way to the interior of the ship, the main part—or middle section—of the ship was just a big open space. A few timbers and beams were scattered here and there to show that there might have been a couple levels of storage there originally, but it was all gone now. Eaten away and decayed by the ocean and currents.

His guys were all sent to see what artifacts could be found in the main area they'd uncovered.

Several fish flitted to and fro when they disturbed their hiding places, but for the most part, the water stayed calmer and clearer now that they were inside the remnants of the ship and out of the direct rush of the water. It made for a much easier working environment.

While he hadn't found anything himself—probably because he kept getting distracted by watching Kayla—he did see that a couple of his guys had placed items in their bags. That was good. It would thrill Kayla to be sure. And perhaps they would be able to gather more clues about the mystery that surrounded the *Lucky Martha*, whatever treasure she bore, and the lives that were taken here.

A loud, hollow thump echoed and drew his attention back to Kayla. She was pulling on something, so he swam over and offered his muscles.

Sure enough, it appeared to be a hatch of some sort, but it was stuck tight. He motioned for her to move back, and he placed his feet on either side of the door and used both arms to pull—hoping to push with his legs to get enough leverage to make the door come unglued.

Nothing happened. So he tried again.

Then, on the third tug, his muscles screaming, the door loosened and drifted open. The momentum of his tug and push from his legs made his body rush upward in the water until he was upside down looking down into the cavity of the ship.

When his light hit the inside, he sucked in a big breath of air.

Kayla was already pointing and signaling a frenzy of words to him. He couldn't help but see the smile in her eyes.

The legend was true.

The ship was full of gold.

Every muscle in his upper body ached. Lifting underwater with the pressure that came with being more than a hundred feet below the surface made it even more difficult to move things. And they had a lot to move.

After their discovery in the hold, the plan had changed. They all resurfaced with everything they had collected, and he and his guys had gone to set up the equipment needed to lower a basket a hundred or more feet into the water. They would still have to haul all of the gold out of the ship by hand, but they would at least be able to fill the basket and let the winch haul it up and out of the water. It would probably take a couple of days, but Steven and his team would handle that while Kayla searched for more artifacts in other sections of the boat or worked back in her lab on all the things that were covered in more than 170 years of concretions and scale growth.

On their way back to the surface on the last dive of the day, Steven swam next to Kayla.

They worked well together. Communicated with their facial expressions and hands better than most people did with words. Not only did he feel a good foundation of trust between them but a budding friendship. One that he hoped to turn into a deeper relationship.

He couldn't rush it. Maybe once they were done with this project, he could ask her out. Officially on a date. He'd only known her a couple of weeks, but because he had a penchant to overthink absolutely everything, he'd already covered every scenario his brain could come up with.

The decision was simple: she was someone he could envision spending the rest of his life with.

One thing needed to be addressed though. . .her faith. He knew she went to church. He'd seen the Bible on the coffee table in her home. But he wasn't sure where she really stood. Because as interesting and kind as Kayla Richardson was, his discernment kept picking up the notion that she had some kind of wall around her heart. He hadn't figured out why, but over time he hoped she would feel comfortable enough to share with him. Hopefully he would have the time with her to build that kind of relationship.

When they reached the surface and climbed out of the water, he took off his mask and breathed deep of the salty air. Something about that first big breath always made him feel more alive.

Kayla smiled at him. "I always love my first breath back at the surface."

"I was just thinking the same thing. Great minds. . ."

She climbed up into his dive boat and squeezed the water out of her hair. "There's not many people I've ever been able to work with like you, Steven. So yeah. . .I agree with you. Great minds." Her light laugh made him smile.

"Hey, I was wondering if you wanted to grab some takeout and go through the items in the box again. I have to admit, you've gotten me hooked on all this historical stuff."

Stepping toward him, she poked him in the chest. The grin on her face almost as wide as the look in her eyes. "I knew it! Even had a bet going with my assistant about how long it would take you to admit that."

"Really?" Was he that easy to guess?

"Yep." Slipping out of her oxygen tanks and gear, she narrowed one eye at him. "And I just won the bet."

"I didn't realize I was that predictable."

"Predictable? Eh. . .maybe not predictable. But I am getting pretty good at reading you. And anticipating your next move. Like I said, we work well together."

They helped the other guys into the boat and stowed gear for the next several minutes.

As he drove the boat back to the dock, he hoped their conversation meant that they were going to move forward. Because he would like nothing more. Although he normally was a very patient man, sometimes even a procrastinator, this was one area of his life that he wanted to rush ahead.

At the dock, all his team grabbed the gear and said their goodbyes. Danny waved at him. "I'll catalog everything back at the office, Boss. See ya tomorrow."

"Sounds good." Steven turned to Kayla, "Anything you need my help with?"

She scanned the boat and checked everything she had in her

arms. "Nope. But I'll take you up on that offer of food and assistance going through the box. The translator's notes came back on the journal, and I'm dying to get a closer look."

"You got a deal. Burritos?"

"You read my mind. Extra cheese, please."

"There's a great taqueria on the way to your place. Let me run home, shower, and change, and I'll be right over."

"Guac and queso?" She hopped onto the dock and looked over her shoulder. "Pretty please?"

"I guess that means you wants chips too?"

"Yep. And for all your trouble, I just *might* send you home with a jar of my homemade salsa."

He groaned in anticipation. "You make your own salsa? I may not be any help at all, because my weakness is chips and salsa."

"I've worked on the recipe for years. It's a secret. And only a few special people ever get to take a jar home."

"I am at your service, miss. I'll do pretty much anything for good salsa." They walked to the parking lot with the remainder of the gear, and he wished he could stretch out every moment with her. Their camaraderie was easy. Comfortable. As if they were always on the same page. Yet he felt it would take a lifetime to get to know every facet of her. Every secret. Every mystery.

"You've got a deal. See you in an hour?"

"Less, if I have anything to do with it. I'm hungry."

She laughed so hard she stopped in her tracks. "I'll be waiting. Just don't forget the extra cheese."

Kayla

Queso dripped from the chip into her hand. Good thing they were sitting at her table; otherwise she'd have her dinner all over her lap and probably the couch and carpet too.

They laughed together and moaned over the amazing flavors and said *yum* more times than she had counted. All in all, it was the best dinner she'd had in a long time. Funny how the meals with Steven all ranked up there like that. Not since her parents had been alive had she felt this way.

The burritos were huge. Almost as big as a football, just maybe not quite that fat. He'd gotten three with grilled chicken and all the fixings, and three with grilled steak. So she'd taken half of one of each. Which was a lot of food. But Steven had already finished two burritos. Plus a bag of warm, homemade tortilla chips, a container of queso, and a half jar of her salsa. All by himself. It was a good thing he'd bought three bags of chips and five containers of the creamy, spicy cheese dip, or she wouldn't have had any.

She glanced up at him as she raised the burrito back up to her mouth. "Not to sound critical or anything—because I don't think there's anything wrong with it—but your food bill must be through the roof."

Steven's eyes twinkled at her as he chuckled around the food in his mouth. "You have no idea. Wanna take an educated guess?"

Squinting at him, she stuck out her lips and thought about it for a moment. "Eight hundred dollars. A month."

"Close." He almost inhaled the next bite, chewed, and swallowed. "A thousand."

Her eyes went wide. "Wow."

"I know. Pretty shocking."

She ate another chip smothered in queso and leaned back in her seat. "That. Was. Amazing. Thank you."

"You're welcome." He began to clean up the remnants of his tornado-style eating.

"I'm so full, I feel like I might need to run a few miles to burn off some of the calories." Getting up from her chair, she began to take care of the few leftovers. "I'll just stick this in the fridge."

"Sounds good. I might need a snack later."

Laughing, she shook her head at him. "Why doesn't that surprise me?"

"Hey, at least you know the truth about me. Most people just stare in shock and don't know what to do."

"Well, there's plenty more salsa to keep you stocked up for the night." She brushed her hands together and wiped off the counters. "Ready to take a look at the journal? I can't wait to see what it holds."

"You bet. Let me grab another glass of tea, and I'll be ready."

She went into the living room and sat on the couch, pulling the journal and translated notes into her lap.

Steven joined her and looked at the box on the coffee table. He picked it up and put it next to him. "I'll keep that close in case we need to check out any of the articles."

"Good thinking." She stretched her legs out to the table and propped up her feet. "All right. Let's see what we've got here." Opening the journal to the first page, she read the first page of translation. She leaned closer to Steven and shifted the papers toward him so they could read at the same time. A couple minutes passed as they read the first entry, which was several pages long.

"Wow. That's quite a story. He comes to America to start a new life. The Depression hits and things spiral downward, but he meets Margo and falls in love." Steven tapped the page. "He got a job working as a diver for the crew building the bridge, and look!" He went to the box and pulled out the article about the celebration on February 26. "He asked her to marry him on this day."

She put a hand to her chest. "That's so sweet. Now I want to know more about them."

"Me too." He put his feet up on the coffee table as well. While her feet were on the edge, his legs went a good foot and a half past hers.

It made her giggle.

He shrugged. "I've got long legs."

"I noticed." She tried not to blush.

"And you've got baby feet." He wiggled his toes, which only accentuated how much bigger his feet were than hers.

"Hey, I like the size of my feet." The look in his eyes almost did her in. It didn't help that they were sitting quite close on the couch. With a breath, she looked back to the translated pages. "Let's read what happens next."

Over the next two hours, they read the whole first half of the journal. The man's hopes and dreams. His fascination with the work as a diver. And the complications of working in the waters of the strait.

"You know, I can't imagine working in these waters back then. With how much the equipment weighed and how hard it would have been to use their gloved hands to get anything done. I am amazed." She shook her head again.

"Yeah, we're pretty spoiled by the technology of today."

"Those guys must have been tough as nails." Going back to the pages, she glanced at how much was left. "Would you like some coffee to make it through? That is, if you're even up for reading the rest?"

"I'm—"

Her phone played the ringtone "Overcomer." "Sorry. Excuse me for a minute." Glancing at the home screen, the number registered the police department. From home. Her heart picked up its pace as she slid the bar to the right to answer. "Hello?"

"Miss Richardson?"

"Yes."

"This is Detective Collins. I'm the one in charge of your mother's case."

Springing up from the couch, she felt a rush of heat fill her body as she headed to the kitchen. "Yes, I know who you are."

"We have an update for you. Our men pulled a vehicle out of Lake Cachuma earlier this week. There was evidence that it had been in a pretty severe accident. After analysis, we've determined that it was the vehicle that hit your mother's car."

Closing her eyes, she bit her lip to keep the tears from coming forward. With a shaky breath, she cleared her throat. "Does that mean you know who killed my mother?"

The man sighed. "Not exactly. We know who the owner of the vehicle is, but we haven't found them yet."

"And once you do?"

"We will investigate and keep you in the loop as to the progress." He paused, and she held her breath as she waited for his next words.

"And?"

"I'm afraid that's all we know at this time, ma'am. If the vehicle was stolen, we may never know because the water did wash away any fingerprints."

"Couldn't you see if there's any DNA?" Couldn't these guys do their job? It had been too long. She needed to know. Needed closure.

"As of right now, we haven't found any. It's been underwater too long. But the forensics team is still searching. Rest assured, Miss Richardson, we are doing everything in our power."

Tears clogged her throat. She'd heard that line so many times. Taking deep breaths, she closed her eyes and pinched the bridge of her nose with her fingers. She could hear Johnathon's voice in her head telling her to let go. But how could she at a time like this?

"Ma'am?"

"I'm here." She leaned against the counter as the weight of the news pressed down on her shoulders. "Thank you for letting me know."

"I'll be in touch as soon as I know anything else."

"Of course." She bit her tongue so she wouldn't say anything she would later regret.

"Have a good night." The detective hung up.

A good night. How could she have anything of the sort after that kind of news?

She hadn't even noticed how he had gotten there, but Steven was standing beside her. "Are you okay?"

His tone of voice and the look in his eyes shattered the carefully erected wall she'd built around herself. The tears she'd tried to hold at bay sprang forth, and a sob escaped her throat. "No. No, I'm not."

His arms slowly came around her shoulders, and without hesitation, she moved into them and cried into his chest.

The grandfather clock in the hall—one of her mother's prized possessions—ticked the seconds as her grief engulfed her. She buried her face in his shirt and sobbed like a baby.

When the clock struck the hour, she was exhausted and completely drained. But there was something so comforting about being in this man's arms.

Not just any man. Steven. The man she trusted. Her friend.

The admission made her want to cry all over again. Since her parents' deaths, she hadn't been able to have any relationships. She'd even managed to push away her longtime friends. Oh, some of them would probably come back in a heartbeat if she asked them, but she didn't have the heart to do it. She'd been empty for too long.

Now. . .even though she felt emptier than ever, she also felt hope. Actual care for another human being. She wasn't cold and isolated anymore.

The wall had been torn down.

Wouldn't Johnathon get a kick out of that?

"Wanna tell me about it?" Steven's chin rested on top of her head, and she found comfort in how his voice vibrated through her whole being.

With a brief nod, she pulled back. "I guess I'd better. A guy deserves an explanation when a girl randomly falls apart and soaks his hoodie with her tears."

He tucked her under his right arm and guided her back to the sofa. "Sit."

She did and tucked her feet up under her.

He handed her a pillow and then kissed her forehead.

The sweet gesture made her want to give in to her tears again.

"Let me get you a glass of water, and you can gather your thoughts." As he walked out of the room, he picked up the box of tissues off the end table and handed it to her.

It only took him a few seconds and he was back. Her apartment really wasn't all that big.

She blew her nose and mopped up her face. "Sorry about your sweatshirt."

"Don't worry about it." He sat next to her. Close. Then he put his arm around her and pulled her against his chest. "Seems like you need a hug right now."

She nodded against him. "I do." Sniffing, she swiped at her eyes again. "I actually can't tell you the last time I had one." The tears started all over again. "I'm sorry." She sobbed.

"Nothing to apologize for. There's no rush. You take all the time you need." He gently stroked the top of her head.

"My mother was killed in a hit-and-run accident eighteen months ago."

He took a long, deep breath. "I'm so, so sorry."

Her head rested against his chest—which was good because she was certain she wouldn't be able to handle looking into his eyes at the moment. The comfort of feeling his depth of concern for her made her want to open up and tell him everything. Something she hadn't done. With anyone.

Ever.

Without saying a word, he kept stroking her hair, twisting the long strands in a slow, rhythmic motion. It was very calming.

"They never caught whoever it was that hit her. It was a direct hit into the driver's door. Her car was pushed into the ditch, and it rolled down the hill. The coroner said she was killed instantly and didn't suffer."

Sucking in another long breath, she then blew it between her teeth, trying to steady her voice. But it cracked and squeaked anyway. "My father died of a heart attack a few weeks later. The doctors said that his heart had been under stress for a while. That he'd been on medication because of it. But I know that it was the stress and heartbreak of losing my mom that killed him. It drove him nuts that they couldn't find who hit Mom. He frantically searched. Went to the police department every day. But they always sent him home. Told him to get counseling. Told him to grieve with me."

Silence stretched as she gathered her thoughts. "Six weeks after Mom was killed, I'd buried both of my parents and hadn't slept for about a week. I'd lost fifteen pounds. After wandering in a fog for a few days, I finally decided that I had to do something about it. So I took up the mantle of my dad's search. Bugged the police several times a day. I'll admit it—I was obsessed with finding who had killed my mother. . .and, in essence, my father too. My work suffered. And my boss sent me to a counselor, telling me that I wouldn't be cleared to dive unless I did." She swallowed and fidgeted with the fringe of her sweater sleeve.

"Did it help?"

"Not really. At least. . .not for the first year. Oh, I did enough to stay cleared to do my job. But I felt like I was just paying him to do that—keep my job."

He took another deep breath, and she listened to his heartbeat. "Let me ask you something. . . . It might be too personal."

"Go ahead."

"Is the counselor a Christian?"

"Funny you should ask. Last time I was there, I knew that my mom would have told me to see my pastor instead because, no, Johnathon isn't a Christian."

"Ah."

"Yeah. So he's completely coming at this from the world's view of healing." She made little quote signs in the air. "For a long time, that was good enough for me because I was keeping my job and content to keep the wall around my grief. But recently I've begun to feel differently."

"How so?"

"I really do want to learn how to let it go. I tried but wasn't successful on my own. Then this job came, and I was content to pour myself into something else. Until we found the skeleton and something about it—probably the fact that the guy was murdered—brought up all the anger and dissatisfaction of the past. I had this insatiable desire to find the killer. Then the nightmares came back." She swiped a hand down her face. She hadn't meant to disclose that much.

"And now?"

"Now?" She sat up and stared into his ever-changing eyes. "I feel lost. Alone. Tired. But I really want it all to be over. I've begged God for all this time to just let me know. I need answers. I want to move on. But I feel broken. Like I'll never be able to truly heal."

He reached out and grabbed her hand. "You're not broken, Kayla. You're stuck. Because you need to grieve. You need to remember that you are a beloved child of God. And you're not alone." He rubbed circles on the back of her hand with his thumb. "I'm here."

Chapter 13

Margo
March 28, 1933

Waking up in her husband's arms was the dream she'd always hoped for. But as she shook off the cobwebs of sleep and stretched in the bed, the reality of their lives crept in again. What she wouldn't give to be able to leave San Francisco right now. Put all of it behind them.

Run away. Then everything would be perfect.

But they had responsibilities. And that meant she had to be here. With someone sending threatening notes. At least for a little while longer.

"Good morning, my love." Luke kissed the top of her forehead. "Why are you so tense this morning?"

Not exactly what she wanted her new husband to notice. He didn't need the added stress of knowing how much this whole thing disturbed her. "Just have a lot on my mind. I have a lot to accomplish today."

"Are you afraid to go to work?"

She sat up in the bed and turned her back to him. "No. I will be fine." Grimacing, she hoped the lie could be forgiven. Hadn't she already told him how much she was on edge? How afraid she was? Just because they were married and she now bore his last name didn't mean that everything all of a sudden was fixed.

"Listen, with all the equipment damaged and no suits for

diving, we will not be going down in the water anytime soon. Whoever it is that sent the notes—if they truly know what is going on—should know that too. Perhaps we will be able to leave before any more dives happen. Then we should be safe. No more threats."

If only she could believe that were true. "I know. And I have to leave it in the Lord's hands." But even as she said the words, her fears grew. "I need to get ready for work. The children wake pretty early." She got up from the bed and headed to the bathroom. Just two more weeks. She could make it that long.

Dressing for the day, she felt an ache building in her chest. To think that just a few short weeks ago, they were dreaming of their lives here. In San Francisco. Forever.

But now that was gone. All because of the gold. If they didn't need it so much, she'd tell Luke to chuck it back into the ocean. But that would be foolish. Times were very difficult.

And someone else knew.

The thought made her shiver.

As soon as she got to the Albrights' home, she questioned if she could even make it two more weeks. No longer did she feel safe. Not in this city. Not at work. Not even at home with Luke.

And by the end of the day, she wasn't even sure she could make it through tomorrow. Everywhere she went, the hair on her neck prickled. She couldn't live like this.

When she got back to Luke's room—their room—she threw herself on the bed and sobbed until she was completely exhausted. That was where Luke found her.

"Margo? Margo? What is wrong?" He sat beside her on the bed and rubbed her back.

Sucking in her bottom lip, she sat up and fell into his arms. "I can't do this. I can't. We have to leave. Soon."

"Why?" He took her face in his hands and made her look him

in the eye. "Did someone hurt you?"

She shook her head and sniffed as tears streamed down her face and over his fingers.

He gently wiped at them. "Oh my love. What is it? What did I do? I am so sorry."

"You didn't do anything wrong." It was true. She couldn't blame him. He was doing his best. "But everywhere I go—I feel like someone is watching me. Following me. I feel their eyes on me. I can't eat. Can't sleep. I'm afraid to take the children anywhere. I don't know what to do anymore. We need to leave."

He let his hands fall to his side. "This is all my fault." He looked exhausted too. "It is my job to keep you safe, and I have failed if you do not feel safe."

"It's not your fault that someone sent those threats, Luke. I don't blame you. I don't. But I'm begging you. Please. We need to leave. No more gold hunting. No more dives. We just need to leave."

He nodded and pulled her back into his arms. He whispered against her hair. "I already put in my notice. So as soon as Mrs. Albright's mother comes to take care of the children, we will leave. I will do my best to explain to my boss and hope that he will still give me a reference." He leaned back and put his hands on the sides of her face again. "Do not go anywhere tomorrow with the children. I will walk you to and from their house—"

"But that will take so—"

"No. It will not be difficult for me. I can walk the extra distance and still have plenty of time. No arguments. Let me take care of you, Margo. Forever."

"Forever." Tears started up again, but she forced a smile.

Everything would be fine.

She had Luke. Forever.

Luke
March 29, 1933

By some miracle, the city had acquired new dive suits in record time.

Their foreman had found George and him at the end of the day to share the good news and tell them that they were first on the docket to dive tomorrow morning. There was likely a lot of cleanup to be done in the area where the charges had blown. And they would probably need to place more charges to be able to get the seafloor ready for the footings of the south tower. They were on a tight schedule and already far behind.

But all of this presented a big problem. Luke had promised Margo that they would leave. And that they would be safe because there wasn't any way to dive and thus make the culprit angrier at them. What was he supposed to do now? Especially since he'd lied to Margo. He hadn't talked to his boss. Not yet. In fact, he was on his way to speak to him when his foreman caught him.

George slapped him on the back. "This is our perfect opportunity."

"What do you mean?" The weight of everything made him feel like he couldn't take a full breath.

"We should dive tonight. See if we can find any more gold."

His head wagged back and forth. "I do not believe that is a good idea."

"Why not?"

"I told you about the notes. Someone is watching us. Knows what we found."

George huffed. "Look, I have a family too. A family that needs food in their bellies and shoes on their feet. I know this is scary, but nobody knows that we have a way to dive."

He stared at the ground.

"I know you're thinking about leaving. The wife is hounding me to leave too. As soon as I told her about the notes you got." He stepped even closer. Tapped his shoulder.

Luke glanced up at his friend.

"Let's go down one more time. See if we can even find the ship if the charges didn't blow it out into the ocean. It'll be the last time. We can get whatever we can. . .then move away. No one needs to know. I know you've heard the rumors. But it's not a curse. I believe—and even my wife believes—that this is a special gift from above. A way for us to find our way in dark times." George ran a hand through his hair. "I know it sounds desperate. But this might be the only chance we have. A chance to give our families a better future."

Luke studied his friend. Desperate times did make men do desperate things. And hadn't God blessed him with finding the ship in the first place? It obviously *was* a gift from heaven. Not a curse. What George said made sense. They could do this. And then leave. "I will do this. One last time."

"One last time." George smiled.

Hours later, after he'd sent a note home to Margo through Mrs. Crispin's grandson, Luke and George stood on the newly engaged dive swing while Charlie ran the controls. They gave him the thumbs-up signal, and down they went.

The water was relatively calm. In fact, it was the quietest he'd ever seen it. An eerie calm made him uncomfortable. All the way down, his thoughts went back and forth like a giant pendulum. One minute the excitement about finding more gold gave him the boost and energy he needed. The next he was worried about who might be watching above the surface of the water. Would they know? Would they go after Margo?

When their lights hit the hull of the ship, amazement hit him. The blasts had cleared away much of the mud and ocean floor that had covered the ship for decades. The thought of this ship being a part of such grand history as the gold rush hit him in the gut. How many men had died hungry and poor because they had spent everything they had in the quest for gold? While some struck it rich, others suffered.

Just like so many suffered now. The financial hardships during the Great Depression affected everyone. Well. . .almost everyone. Margo was right. If they found a lot of treasure, they needed to help others with it. Not just themselves.

Luke vowed then and there to use what he found for good. To help others.

George headed for the ship and the clear hole where they'd ventured before. It didn't take long before they found several more nuggets of gold. Big nuggets too.

Time running short, Luke searched the bottom level of the ship. There had to be another compartment here somewhere.

After several minutes, he found a hatch! Pulling with all his might, he yanked and tugged until he felt it give. Then it opened.

Giddy as a child waiting to open a present on Christmas morn, he peered down into the hole.

The empty eye sockets of a skeleton stared back and made him rush back as fast as he could. Running into George, he reminded himself to breathe and pointed to the open hatch.

His friend took a glance and jerked even more than Luke had.

Taking several moments to compose himself, he went back to the hatch. The man was bound in chains. There was a box in between his hands. And more gold than he'd ever seen underneath the skeleton.

Luke worked to pull the box free. He tried to open it but couldn't underwater. He'd have to bring it up with him.

George helped him to move the skeleton out of the hold. It felt very disrespectful to disturb the man's grave. No matter how violent a death he must have suffered, he deserved peace now. But the gold beckoned them both.

Putting the box back into a corner of the hold, Luke motioned to George, and they went to work. Grabbing what they could, they filled their nets. It was enough for them to have fresh starts. Wherever they chose to go. He took one last glance at the hold. There was enough gold down here to make more trips than they could count. For days. That was from what they could see.

But their time was up, and they climbed onto the swing to be hauled to the surface. Greed was a hideous beast. And he didn't want that. He'd have to look in the box another time.

The whole time up to the surface, Luke couldn't swipe the grin off his face. Wait until Margo saw. He'd hide it in the closet until she was home from helping Amelia. Then he'd tell her they could go wherever they wanted to go.

Of course, they'd give a good portion of it to Charlie and thank him for helping them. But they could leave now. No doubt about that. It still pricked his conscience to leave his boss in a bad way. But there were plenty of other men who needed jobs. There had to be some trained divers among them.

Everything would work out.

The Son

So they'd found it.

They'd better not have taken all his gold. Obviously his notes hadn't scared them enough.

Watching the men hug at the dock, he seethed. No one stole what was rightfully his. No one.

Then an idea formed. It was perfect.

Moving stealthily around the rocky edge, he waited for the men to go into the locker room.

Once they were in, he crawled behind a bush.

The one who'd stayed up top came out first, followed by the wiry man who had the pretty girlfriend. The last one out was the biggest out of all of them.

Maybe he should go for the wiry one. He had the best chance to overpower him.

But the big man shouted to his friends. "I forgot my keys. You go on ahead. I'll see ya tomorrow."

"All right."

"See ya then!"

The other two waved.

Decision made.

The big man would be his target. And since he was all alone, there wouldn't be anyone to help him.

Chapter 14

Flip
July 28, present day

There wasn't any way to get around those patrols.

Pacing his apartment, he wracked his brain. Every idea he had petered out when it ran its course. Nothing would give him access.

Except diving for the city and Miss Kayla Richardson.

He stopped in his tracks.

That was it.

All he had to do was get Steven fired from the restoration job. Then they'd need other divers to help the underwater archaeologist.

He could use that to his advantage. He was experienced.

And she knew him. Trusted him.

Bingo.

Time to dig up some dirt and frame Steven Michaels.

He'd take over the job and have access whenever he wanted.

Problem solved.

Kayla
July 29, present day

"I need to speak with Dr. Langston, please." She knew he was there. Waiting for her.

"One moment, please." The receptionist put her on hold.

The music was soothing and soft. A beautiful piece with cello and piano.

"This is Dr. Langston."

"Johnathon. It's Kayla."

"Running a bit behind?" His tone was light. Nonaccusatory.

"Actually, I'm not coming this evening." She didn't feel an ounce of guilt.

"Oh?"

"But I want to continue. I think I've made some good progress. The detective on my mom's case called. I spent the night crying and hashed it out with a good friend." Is that *all* Steven was? While it was definitely wonderful to have him as a friend, she realized she wanted more. Much more.

"That is good to hear. When would you like to reschedule?"

"Tomorrow?"

"Same time?"

"Yes. But I do have one condition."

He cleared his throat. "That's not how I do things, Kayla. You know how unhealthy—"

"Please. Hear me out."

A long pause. "All right."

"I haven't been honest with you about everything. I've tried to keep all of this separate from my faith, and that just won't work anymore. I need you to know that I'm going to be seeing a pastor as a counselor too. And I need you to listen to me unbiased as I share about what I believe." She swallowed and then took a sip of water. "Can you do that?"

"Of course, Kayla. I don't think you need two counselors, but if it makes you feel better, I'm on board. There will be no judgment from me. My father was a man of faith. And just because I didn't follow in his footsteps doesn't mean I don't respect those who do."

She let out her breath in a whoosh. "Thank you."

"See you tomorrow?"

"Tomorrow." She hung up the phone. That had gone better than she'd hoped.

Why had she shoved her faith aside? It wasn't until Steven entered her life that she realized that she'd even done it. Of course, when she thought about it, it made sense. She'd shoved everything and everyone aside. Like she was a racehorse with blinders on. Barreling toward the finish line no matter what stood in her way.

Her buzzer rang, and she jumped up to speak into the intercom. "Hello?"

"Hey. It's me." Steven's voice washed over her and made her smile.

"Come on up." She buzzed him through the outer door and then went to unlock her door and open it. It felt. . .*right* to be so comfortable around him.

"Hey there. I brought food!" He came in and took off his shoes and then pushed the door shut with his foot. "Surprise, surprise."

"Of course you did. When do you *not* bring food? Or talk about food?"

"Touché." He held out three plastic sacks holding brown paper bags.

"Is that what I think it is?"

"I don't know. Do you think it's takeout from Original Joe's?"

It made her laugh. "Yes! Exactly what I was going to guess. It's perfect." She'd told him it was her favorite that first night they ate together.

"Good. Because I brought the whole menu. Well, maybe not the *whole* menu. But almost all of it. We've got prosciutto and burrata, Joe's meatballs, garlic bread, Dungeness crab cocktail, a couple of prime New York steaks, fettuccine Alfredo, and ravioli."

"And brownies?" She bounced on her toes.

"Of course. I would *not* forget their double fudge brownies. Especially after you raved about them."

They worked in tandem, grabbing plates, silverware, and drinks, and spread out the food on the table.

"So. . .what are we gonna work on tonight?" He passed her a napkin.

"The rest of the journal?"

"Sounds good to me. I had to admit, I've been wondering what happened to Mr. Moreau and Miss Hunley."

The meal passed in easy conversation. She even told him about her exchange with Johnathon. "You know, I was wondering if you think it would be okay if I asked your pastor to counsel me."

He actually put down his fork. "Sure. I mean, I can't speak for him and what his schedule looks like, but I'm sure Jeremy will make time for you. He only counsels women with his wife present. Let me grab his number for you."

"Thank you. Having another woman's input would be really helpful to me. Ever since I lost my mom. . ." Her words clogged her throat all of a sudden, "I haven't had another woman to talk to."

Her Apple watch dinged.

"There, I just sent you a text with his number." He put his phone down and then picked it back up. "You know, here's his wife's name and number too."

"Thank you."

Conversation flowed so naturally, Kayla couldn't believe she'd been so fortunate to find someone like Steven. And to think that God pretty much plopped the guy right into her lap.

They finished their dinner and dessert and headed back into the living room.

"Thank you for food. Again." She smiled and got up to take care of the mess.

"Let me help." Between the two of them, it took only a few

minutes to put leftovers away and clean up the table. Then they took their same positions on the couch, and she opened the journal back to where they left off.

Blinking several times, she tried to work the dryness from her eyes.

"Here, let me read to you for a bit. That way you can rest your eyes."

He had to be the most caring and observant man on the planet.

As he read through the entries, the ordinary life of Luke Moreau seemed more and more extraordinary. She found herself wanting to cheer the sweet couple on as if she were watching a movie of their lives.

She got up to refill their waters.

"Oh, hurry back. Listen to this." Steven pointed to where they were in the journal. "'Today I had the most incredible discovery. The tidal currents pushed me far from the site where I was supposed to be. Before I knew what was happening, I was slammed into the ocean wall. Or so I thought. The water cleared for only a moment, and I thought I saw the outline of a ship. Then something else caught my eye. It was a gold nugget—'"

"He must be talking about the *Lucky Martha*!" She bounced on the couch. "Keep reading. Hurry."

Over the next couple of hours, they lost all track of time as they pored over the journal entries. Not only had Luke found the ship and some gold, but he went down to it several times. They came to a mention of some notes that threatened Margo and him. And the whole mood of the journal changed.

What had been full of hope and joy was now overshadowed by obsession with the gold—whether he should be trying to get more—and revealed his greatest fears and worries.

Several entries later, Steven paused. She leaned closer and read silently.

Luke had found a skeleton too! Wrapped in chains!

She covered her mouth with her hand.

"It's got to be the skeleton you wrestled with." Steven's sideways smirk made her release her breath and laugh.

"Wrestled with. Yeah, thanks for the reminder." She shook her head. "But you're right. It's got to be the same person." She leaned closer to his side. "Keep reading."

The skeleton had been holding a box that Luke wanted to look at, but then he and his friend George found a lot of gold, and hid the box back in the hold. Inwardly, she continued to cheer for the hero of the story. A real life story. Hm. What was in the box?

But then the journal turned cryptic. Fewer details. No more mention of what he planned to do. No mention of the notes or the ship again.

Then it abruptly stopped.

Steven let out a sigh. "That's it."

Kayla turned to sit sideways on the couch so she was facing him, her legs tucked up under her. "I have this horrible, sinking feeling in my stomach." She put her hand over the offending area.

"Too much brownie?"

She swatted his arm. "No. But I appreciate you always trying to make me laugh."

"That's what I'm here for."

She rolled her eyes at him. "What if. . ." Pinching her lips together, she almost didn't want to voice her thoughts aloud. As if it would make them real. And she really, really didn't want them to be true.

"What?"

"The threatening notes. The tone of his journal entries at the end. The abrupt end. His disappearance."

"Yeah. . ." He prodded her on to finish the thought.

"What if. . . I mean. . . Do you think the other set of bones could belong to Luke?"

All night he'd thought about Kayla's question. Even his dreams were filled with it. As much as he hated to admit it, he realized she just might be right.

Luke Moreau must have died down with the ship.

Or could he have been murdered as well? The threatening notes didn't bode well.

It made him think about Margo. Would there be any record of her anywhere? There had to be a way to look. Especially with the tech they had today. Everyone was searching their family trees nowadays.

Another idea hit. What if he tried to find her on social media? Someone out there had to know something about her. A relative? He could get his networking guy to work on that tomorrow.

He'd love to see Kayla's face if he were to present her with a clue about Margo Hunley.

Kayla.

The woman was a mystery, a fascination, and a thorn in his side all at the same time.

Well, he couldn't really call her a true thorn in his side, not really. It's not like she irritated him or drove him up the wall. But man, what he wouldn't give to be able to tell her how he felt right now.

In fact, he'd thought several times about calling Dad and telling him that he'd met the woman he wanted to marry.

Shaking his head, he huffed. *That* wasn't something he wanted to say to her just yet. She'd probably run away screaming.

But in his heart, he knew. Dad would understand. He said he knew he was gonna marry Mom the day they met.

The man had an intellect like his own. Loved to think and plan then think some more. They teased each other about overthinking everything. About how many brain cells they'd killed by blowing fuses running over the same ideas and problems so many times.

While he wanted to call his dad and tell him everything, he had to get to work. There were way too many questions and not enough answers.

The mystery surrounding the *Lucky Martha* was multifaceted. It wasn't just a ship that went down during the gold rush. It wasn't just a ship that was surrounded by legends—carrying a cargo no one knew about and mysterious origins and owners. Now it was also the site of a murder. Possibly two. . .or more.

What had *really* happened during the building of the Golden Gate Bridge? Why had those men quit and/or disappeared?

For a guy who loved diving and restoration work, he sure was interested in the history of it all now. The thought made him smile.

The work that Kayla did was more interesting than his own.

For the hundredth time, he thought about changing fields of work.

When he made it to the mayor's office, he glanced at his watch. He was only a minute late. Good thing his long legs could cover the distance in a short amount of time.

"Glad you could make it, Mr. Michaels." Mayor Riley frowned at him.

Steven looked over at Kayla. She shrugged. The mayor was normally all smiles. Especially if there were cameras around.

He winced. That wasn't fair. Just because he didn't like the mayor's style didn't mean the man didn't have a legitimate reason to be agitated with him for his tardiness.

Taking his seat behind the desk, the mayor looked at some notes from a folder and then abruptly closed it. With his hand on top, he stared at it. "I'm afraid I've been made aware of derogatory statements—some allegations—that will be printed in the evening edition of today's paper. It will also run on the evening news. After much consideration, I'm afraid I'm going to have to have my people investigate."

Kayla leaned forward in her seat. "Derogatory statements? About me?" She had a hand on her chest. Her cheeks were pink. Surely no one would bring up her mother's death and the circumstances surrounding it.

Mayor Riley held up a hand. "No, Kayla. It's nothing about you." He narrowed his gaze at Steven. "I'm afraid this is about Mr. Michaels."

That wasn't what he was expecting. "What?"

"An anonymous tip has been given about a bridge collapse. A bridge that your team did the restoration on."

"Wait. I'm confused." Steven furrowed his brow. "The only bridge that my company did restoration on that collapsed was because of an earthquake."

"Exactly. According to this document, your team covered up the collapse with the earthquake when it really was because of inadequate and faulty design."

"That is a false accusation." Steven shook his head. He stood behind his team and their work. He double- and triple-checked every job. Every bolt. Every piece of bracing. Every inch of concrete.

The mayor tilted his head. "While I would like to take your word on the matter, you must understand the predicament I find myself in."

"Which is?"

"Whether you should be allowed to continue to assist Miss Richardson on the project until we find out the truth. This isn't just about your reputation or your company, Mr. Michaels. You are assisting Miss Richardson and she is working for the city. On a project that is worth millions and could be the largest historical find of the century. The city's reputation is at stake. Integrity is everything."

Steven stood up from his chair. "Sir. This is outrageous. Surely you can see that an anonymous tip cannot be trusted as a source. We have verification from three different sources that the cause of that bridge collapse was the earthquake." He looked over at Kayla. He couldn't read her expression. What was she thinking? She wouldn't believe the accusation, would she?

"Nevertheless, I think maybe it's best if you do not dive with Miss Richardson for a few days. Until we can be assured that everything is above board."

"What about my team? She needs all the hands she can get, and my guys are trained and know the job."

The mayor shook his head. "I'm sorry. No. Especially after the fiasco with the gear the other day. Well I'm sorry. I'm sure all of this will be cleared up soon enough. We will hire another team to help Kayla."

Kayla came to her feet at that. "While that is very generous, Mr. Mayor, that isn't necessary. I won't have the time to train a new crew, and frankly, I don't want to. So I won't be doing anymore diving until this is resolved."

Riley sighed. "I really wish you would reconsider. I don't want any more delays on this project."

She shrugged. "Well, then, maybe you need to find another underwater archaeologist who will sign your confidentiality agreements and be ready at your beck and call for your next publicity stunt."

"Miss Richardson. That is uncalled for." The mayor's face registered his shock. "I have no desire to hire someone else."

"Good. Then get this cleared up. You know how to find me when you have." Without even looking at Steven, she marched out of the room.

Steven didn't know what to think. Was she mad at him? But she did stand up for him. . .kinda. At least she said she didn't want to work with anyone else. That gave him a boost.

But it wasn't much. Because according to the mayor, he was about to be blasted on the news.

"I'm sorry, sir. Rest assured, there is no truth to those allegations."

The mayor came around his desk. "You seem like an honorable man, Steven. I want to believe that. But you have to understand that with the city's money at stake, I have to ensure that everything is on the up and up."

"I understand that, sir, but I wish it wasn't *my* reputation that was about to smeared. Integrity is everything to me." As the depth of it all hit him square in the chest, he took a deep breath. "Excuse me."

"Of course."

He was out the door in a couple of seconds and ran down the hall, down the stairs, and out the door. He had to catch Kayla.

There. She was opening her driver door.

"Kayla!" He reached her in six long strides. "Thank you for what you said back there."

Her eyes shot daggers at him. "I meant what I said, Steven. I don't want to work with another team. But trust is hard for me. After all we've shared the past week. . ." She looked away and swallowed. "I thought you understood that honesty is everything to me. Truth at all costs."

"Me too." Didn't she know that?

"You need to tell me. Did your team have anything to do with that bridge's collapse?"

"No." His word was emphatic.

"All right." She put her hands on the wheel. "I'm sorry. I need to process."

"Okay. May I call you later?"

"I don't know. . . . You can try." Shifting her Bug into gear, she drove away. Without a glance back or anything.

What had just happened?

Chapter 15

Luke
March 29, 1933

After a long, hot shower, Luke headed back to his room and his wife, his hair dripping into the towel around his neck.

Mrs. Crispin came up the stairs. "Mr. Moreau."

"Yes?"

"You have a visitor." She didn't look very happy about it. Especially since she locked the doors and her curfew for all her tenants was in four minutes.

"Thank you, ma'am." He raced down the stairs, wondering who on earth it could be. Maybe one of the guys forgot something?

But when he went out the door, his couldn't help but gasp. "George? What happened to you?" His eyes were swollen and bloodshot, and bruises had begun to form all over his face.

"We're in a bit of trouble."

"I can see that." His stomach fell to his feet. "We need to get you cleaned up. I can call a doctor."

"No. No doctors. Don't worry about me at the moment. . .but. . ."

"What is it?"

"The man who did this. . .well, he promises to do worse to our wives if we don't cooperate. He needs our help to dive down and get the rest of the gold. He says it's his."

He looked around the porch and the drive. No one seemed to be around. Even so, he whispered. "Look, let us just leave tonight. We can gather up our families and simply go. Margo has a relative—"

"No." George shook his head as he leaned up against the house and groaned. He licked his cracked lips. "No. He said he's watching us. And not just him. He has more guys. Following us. Everywhere we go. Following Margo and Amelia. He told me about everything my wife has done the past few weeks. Then told me about Margo and the notes he left her. Then he said that all the guys that quit or are missing? He killed them, Luke. They're all dead."

He couldn't wrap his mind around what his friend was saying. It couldn't be true. Would that man really do it? Or was he trying to scare them? "What do I tell Margo? We were planning. . ."

George came forward and grabbed his collar. "We can't tell them anything. He said he will kill them both if we do. He found the gold I brought up tonight. And I told him about the box. But that we didn't bring it up."

His heart drummed faster and faster. He looked up to the second story of the house. "Did you tell him about the other bag that I have?"

"No. I figured we might need that to make our escape. But he doesn't trust us. That's for sure."

"What did he say we have to do?"

"Tomorrow night after work, we have to get Charlie to help, and we will dive down and see if we can get the rest of the treasure."

"Did you tell him how long that's going to take?" Neither of them really knew how much was still there. But from what he'd seen, that would take several days. At least.

"I told him it would take a good bit of time—if we could find the ship each time." He grabbed his shoulder. "Look, I'm in a lot of pain and want to go home. But promise me that you won't take off without me?"

"I promise. I will not leave you, George." Guilt riddled him. It was his fault. If he hadn't taken that first gold nugget. . .then told

George about it. . .

"Thank you. We'll help him get his gold, but he can't take it all. We still have what we've got hidden."

Luke nodded. And after this, they would need it more than ever.

"One thing's for certain. We need a plan. And soon. When we leave here, we can't leave a trace. We have to disappear. For good."

Margo

She placed a bookmark in her Bible and looked at the door. Luke had been gone longer than she anticipated.

The doorknob turned, and she sat up straighter in the bed and put on a smile. She was determined to make the best of it until they left. "There you are."

But his face was haggard looking. "I am sorry, my love. George stopped by with some news."

"Oh?"

"Yes. New dive suits arrived today, so that means we will need to stay later for a few days this week."

"So you're diving again?" She scurried out of the bed and stood. The room chilled her.

"I am afraid so, yes."

"But I thought we were leaving as soon as Mrs. Albright's mother arrived?" He wouldn't go back on his word, would he?

His eyes shuttered closed for a moment, and he swiped a hand through his thick dark hair. It was half dry now from his shower and stood up on end, spiking all over the place. The disarray made her think about her life. It was all in disarray too. Nothing was going like it should.

"I was not anticipating the equipment to arrive so soon. I cannot in good conscience leave until they have a replacement for me."

The fear crept back in. "And they are looking for one?"

"Yes." He looked down at the floor.

He wouldn't lie to her. . .would he?

She wrapped her arms around her waist. Anything to feel safe, secure. She had no more words for him.

Stepping toward her, he held out his arms.

But she put up a hand. "No. Don't try to comfort me now. I can't deal with all this. I'm scared, Luke. You know that. Please. Just do what you have to do, and hurry. I don't know how much more of this I can take."

She turned her back on him and climbed back into the bed, pulling the covers up over her shoulders. Staring at the wall, she prayed that God would help them make it through. Even if her husband was not handling things the way she would choose to, she needed to follow him. They were married now.

But that didn't mean she had to make it easy for him all the time. Sometimes things had to be learned the hard way.

Chapter 16

Kayla
July 31, present day

Morning light streamed in through her wall of windows. It was the reason she had bought the place. Everything in San Francisco cost a fortune. Especially if you wanted any space at all. And windows? You paid through the nose for those too.

But she didn't mind. She loved this city. Even though the culture she'd fallen in love with a decade ago had changed. Once big tech moved in, the art, music, and real culture seemed to slowly fade away.

Of course technology had taken over the world. She used to be able to strike up a conversation with someone while waiting for the bus or other city transit. But now? Everyone was talking on the phone, glued to the screen, or had ear buds stuffed in their ears, which made it easy to ignore the world around them. When she traveled, she saw the same thing everywhere she went. So it wasn't just her beloved city that had been affected by it.

She walked out onto her balcony with her coffee and let the breeze wash over her. The weather here was her favorite. Mild pretty much year-round. She even loved the fog that rolled in most evenings.

Next to that, she loved the diversity. People from all over the world came here to live. She loved that she could hear different languages as she walked down the street. And the festivals. Oh, how she loved the festivals. She could get lost in the street fairs each weekend hosted by different neighborhoods.

Mom had loved going to all of them with her. And Kayla kept up the tradition. Mainly to help her feel connected to her mother, but also because it kept her busy. Helped her stay numb.

But Steven had changed all that.

She'd allowed her walls to come down for him. And she had no idea why. It had felt like a good thing. Until the news yesterday.

It had been one thing to hear the mayor talk about how an anonymous source had alleged something. Another thing entirely to hear the nightly news question the integrity of the man she'd opened up to. . .the man who was her friend. . .the man—sigh—she cared for. Deeply.

While she hated the last words she'd spoken to him yesterday, she needed time. Space. To sort through her feelings. Sort through how she would handle it.

Johnathon had encouraged her yesterday to trust her friend. Wait for all the details and facts to come to light. In fact, they'd spent the entire session talking about Steven.

After debating with herself last night for hours, she'd come to one conclusion. She believed in Steven. Even though her pessimistic brain would love to give in to the doubts and fears. She *did* trust him. She had no reason not to. And as much as honesty meant to her, she couldn't find any reason why he would lie to her. At first she was heartbroken to think that he could be responsible for a bridge collapse. Then she'd gone and read the reports. On top of the fact that she knew Steven. She knew that he didn't cut corners. He prided himself on that.

The accusations had to be false.

They had to be.

Hearing the clock chime, she realized it was time to get going. Today she would dive. By herself. No one needed to know except her assistant, Carrie. She could stay up top while Kayla did some searching on her own. Besides, it was therapeutic for her.

An hour later, she was on the dive platform of the boat, shoving her regulator into her mouth. She gave the signal to Carrie and went into the water. As the sea engulfed her, she closed her eyes for a moment and pushed everything aside. She needed to get rid of all the noise. God hadn't given her a spirit of fear. But He'd given her a spirit of power, love, and a sound mind. She repeated the words.

It had been far too easy to push Steven away. . .just like she'd done with everyone else after Mom and Dad died. But she needed to break that habit. Steven deserved an apology. And she had to stop letting her faith drift whenever things got tough. This wasn't who she was.

But what if the detective came up empty-handed? Again.

She forced those thoughts back. No. She wouldn't allow them to gain control again.

In the long run, it didn't matter if the detective came up with anything.

God knew. He knew how much she hurt. How much she'd closed herself off from others. That was probably why He brought Steven into her life. So she could be alive again.

It was time to lay her burdens down at Jesus' feet.

While Johnathon had tried to convince her to *choose* to let it go, in her heart, she knew that God could carry that burden way better than she could.

If only she wasn't such a control freak. Opening her eyes, she watched the GPS on her dive watch and began to kick her fins. Planning was what she did best. It was her go-to de-stressor. If she could, she'd plan out the rest of her life. If only God would give her a sticky note from heaven about what she was supposed to do next.

After this project was over, what would she do? She hadn't signed any contracts for any other work. Maybe she needed to take a bit of a break.

Allow herself to grieve.

When people had challenged her to do that before, she'd brushed it all aside. She'd always responded by saying that she'd already grieved. She had. She'd been adamant about it. But looking back at the past year, she had to admit she hadn't. Not really.

And that would make Mom sad. She would want Kayla to be facing life with joy. Yes, she'd want to be remembered and treasured. Every mom probably would. But she'd insist that Kayla cherish the memories and move forward with them. Talk about them. Share what Mom had taught her and had loved—cooking, good food, crocheting, a good story, and all the rest—with someone else. As Kayla made her way down to the coordinates where the *Lucky Martha* lay, she could almost hear Mom's voice in her head. "Go. Look forward. Have fun."

How she longed to do that.

Her light caught the rough timber of the bow, and she focused on the ship. *All right, lady. What do you have for me today?*

If she could ask the question aloud, she would. If only the ship could speak back. Normally she loved investigating and finding all the clues that were left behind, but this one really had her befuddled. Probably because she couldn't grasp all the different timelines and what they meant. From 1849 to 1890-something to the 1930s. Too many pieces to the puzzle were missing.

Venturing into the side of the ship, she went over every inch of the big open space. Not much was left, but she went over to the hatch and lifted it. They hadn't actually gone down into the hold before. Just looked at the gold and made a plan. But what if there was something other than gold down there? Luke's diary had mentioned a box.

It was probably lost, but the thought spurred her on because there were probably other items down here that would be fascinating.

She normally didn't like going into tight spaces unless there was someone else with her—just in case—but her curiosity got the best of her.

The hold was full of gold. Her light scanned the area as she moved her head. Pulling her extra flashlight out of her belt, she peered into each corner.

There was more room down here than she'd thought. But as she studied the area, she realized that the bottom of the ship must have busted open during the sinking or had disintegrated over time, because the gold had spilled and covered a much wider area. If it were still within the ship, it would be narrower, not wider.

Getting her light into a far corner, she studied it. She couldn't quite get close enough to make out what the object was. So she pulled out her collapsible mini-shovel and tried to move the gold gently away from the area so she could fit back there.

It took about fifteen minutes, but her persistence paid off. Folding up the shovel again, she shimmied her way into the corner.

Up close, she allowed herself to smile.

The box.

Well, maybe not *the* box that Luke had mentioned, but it was *a* box. And usually these kinds of things held items of significance. She hoped it was true of this one.

Flip

Across the strait, he sat in his boat behind the north tower. This was as close as he could get without the patrols at the south tower recognizing him from the other day and questioning him. Lifting his binoculars, he watched Kayla's boat. Her mousy assistant had stayed up top and kept a careful eye on the water.

While Steven's name was getting slandered as he had devised, Flip hadn't planned on his idea backfiring and Kayla refusing to work with anyone else. The mayor was determined to listen to her and delay the project. That meant they wouldn't be diving. And the patrols would continue. There had to be another way to get down there. But no one was cleared except Kayla. And she had said she wouldn't dive until the mess was cleared up. So why was she down there tonight?

An idea began to form. The question was, could he pull it off—without her?

It was risky. But at this point, it was probably his only shot.

He watched until Kayla surfaced and handed a small object to her assistant. It wasn't anything big. Didn't look like gold. But that didn't matter. It worked into his plan perfectly. The shutter of his camera clicked.

Wouldn't be long now. He'd have the gold. And he'd have his wife back.

Nothing else could stand in his way.

Steven

August 2, present day

He'd answered the same questions at least twenty times now. To at least that many people. He understood that the investigators from the Department of Transportation had to be thorough, but they already had all of his company's files. Every picture, video, and report that they'd made during the restoration. Every inspection report. Every inspection video. Every piece of evidence. So why couldn't they come to a conclusion already? The truth was plain to see. And umpteen witnesses had substantiated it. There wasn't a shred of evidence to prove the anonymous source's claims were true. But whenever the media got involved, an investigation had to be reopened just to put the public at ease. At least that's what he'd been told.

Now the investigators were deliberating, and he'd been sent home to wait. Normally, he was a patient man. But his reputation was on the line. His business was on the line.

And then there was Kayla.

Her reaction wasn't exactly what he'd hoped for. But after he'd had time to walk away and cool off, he couldn't blame her. Not after all she'd gone through. And it's not like they'd really known each other that long. They weren't married. They didn't know anything and everything about each other. So of course she didn't stand behind him and trust every word that came out of his mouth. If he were an observer standing on the outside, he would probably hesitate too. In fact, he knew he would.

But, man, how he wished it were different. He wanted Kayla to believe in him. That was even more important to him than his company. He could start over somewhere else. He could. But there wouldn't be another woman like her. Ever.

Because she was the one.

But it wasn't his situation to control. God had it. And Steven needed to let it remain in His hands. The waiting part was what drove him mad. Of course, God's timeline didn't fit into his own. As much as he tried to make it happen, he would fail every time.

All right, God. I know You've got this. I do. But I'm struggling. He let out a long sigh. *Maybe You're trying to tell me that I need to stop focusing on myself and pray for someone else? Okay. Lord, I lift up my guys to You. I know most of them don't have any faith at all, and I've wanted to be Your Light to them. Help me to do better at that. Father, that brings me to Kayla. Help her heart to grieve and to heal. And if it's Your will, Lord, could you please help the detective bring her answers about her mother's death? I know that would bring her some much-needed closure. I ask that You wrap Your loving arms around her, help her to feel Your love and Your presence. In Jesus' name, I ask all these things.*

Getting up from the sofa, he paced the room. There had to be something else that he could do to pass the time. He needed to contact his networking guy and get the info out about Margo on social media. Maybe they could find something that way. But that wouldn't take long.

What if he made something for Kayla? It had been a long time since he'd worked in his shop. Dad and Grandpa would be proud if he put some of his woodworking skills to use. And it would keep his hands and mind busy. Something he desperately needed right now.

But what could he make?

He scanned his memories of her apartment. He had seen several pictures of dolphins. Of course, everything in her home had a warm feel to it, but the ocean had been a big part of it.

Decision made, he went out to his workshop to search for just the right piece of wood. It wouldn't be easy, but once he had it carved, the time it would take to hand sand it smooth would be good for him. Get some of his nervous energy out.

Time to get to work.

Now if only Kayla would see him again so he could give it to her.

Chapter 17

Luke
April 1, 1933

At this point, stalling was his only option. Luke looked over at George. Two days had passed. Augustus De Ville was frantic to get that gold. Yeah, they'd found out his name. And unfortunately, he knew how to dive. Didn't seem to mind the heavy gear. Everything Luke had come up with so far to deter the man blackmailing them hadn't worked.

Today, during their regular workday, the explosive charges had been loaded into the framework and lowered to the seafloor so the divers could place them again. That meant it was all underway. The only excuse he could think of tonight was that the water would be murky still from the blasts. At least he could hope and pray they were.

He and George had decided to try and keep the man from the ship until they could find a way to get him caught. So far they hadn't figured out a way to do that. But the man was dangerous. Not only had he beat George, but his wife, Amelia, had been scared to death by a man following her around. He'd even grabbed her at one point and told her she'd better tell her husband to listen if he knew what was best for him.

Things were way out of hand. If they helped Augustus, wouldn't he just hurt them worse later? There had to be something they could do to stop him rather than reward him. But they were scared.

Scared to stay. Scared to leave. This wasn't the way to live. And it was all Luke's fault.

Now it was dark, and Charlie was lowering the three of them down into the water. When Luke put up his hand, he couldn't even see it at arm's length. He breathed out a sigh. That meant the good Lord was still churning that water. And with all the blasts today, visibility would hopefully be down to nothing for a day—maybe two.

But to prove to Augustus they were trying, he and George decided that they would pretend to put forth their best efforts. If he wanted frantic, they could definitely do that. Perhaps even argue with each other back up top about who had the best idea to help get it. Whatever it took to prove their sincerity so Augustus would leave their families alone.

When they reached the seafloor, Luke felt the current push him back and off the swing. Back. Back. Without being able to see, his bearings were off. If it pushed him too far, he'd go off the ledge. And not near the ship. They'd placed stakes on the seafloor above the *Lucky Martha* to help lower themselves over the cliff. But they'd intentionally gone to a different location with Augustus, an area they weren't accustomed to. And with nothing to keep him from going over the edge, he could plummet to a dangerous depth.

Leaning forward, he tried to see the others. But they were nowhere to be found. He worked his arms and legs to move forward. Maybe if he could find the swing, he could at least get his bearings. But so far nothing.

Moments like this always presented a bit of panic. But he'd been trained to deal with it. And he could. He took long, calming breaths. Got his heart rate back to a lower rhythm. He didn't want to use up too much air. If he couldn't see anything, then George and Augustus couldn't either. So he stayed put. Closed his eyes and felt the water's movement. If he was correctly gauging which direction it was pushing him now compared to when he first reached the seafloor, he needed to turn a few degrees to his left. Then he could step forward.

One. Two. Three. Four. He still couldn't see anything, but when he reached his arms in every direction, his left arm made contact with something. He grabbed it with his hand. Then he moved his head as close as he could. Peering through the small window in his helmet, he caught sight of one of their swings. Now if he just stayed right here. Or maybe he should signal Charlie to pull him to the surface. But not until he saw George. He couldn't leave without his friend.

An awful thought went through his mind. If he and George made it to the swings, then they could abandon Augustus. Get back to the surface and let the depths take the bad man.

But as soon as he finished the thought, he instantly regretted it. That would not be honoring to the Lord.

He waited for several minutes, scanning the space in front of him for any signs of the other two divers. Then a bump to his right shoulder made him jump. It was Augustus. He saw a bit of terror in the man's eyes as their helmets clashed.

Augustus tugged and gave the signal to be pulled up, but Luke signed to him that they needed George.

The man refused to wait.

Luke wouldn't leave George down here. He'd just have to insist to go back down after Augustus got over his little panic attack. Luke could follow the air line and locate his friend.

But when they reached the surface, George was the one who greeted them. Once they all had taken off their helmets, George charged at Augustus. "You are an idiot! Why didn't you listen when we told you the water was too disturbed? We could have died down there!"

"We're fine. Look. We all made it to the top."

Luke didn't appreciate the cold stare from the man. "But you thought George was still down there. You were perfectly willing to abandon a man."

Augustus narrowed his eyes. "What's it to you? I'm the one in charge here. This is my gold we're after. And if you want to see your pretty wife again, I suggest you stop questioning me." The man moved to walk away as if nothing had happened.

But George charged again and shoved the guy. "I'm not going down there anymore. I'm done."

"You don't get to make that decision."

"Yes, I do. You can't find it without us. And frankly, I don't want you to find it. There's three of us and only one of you." George rose to his full height. He was a big man.

"You do realize that if something happens to me, your families will be killed?"

George flinched for only a moment. Then anger filled his face again. "Why you, dirty—"

Augustus charged him that time and shoved George into the metal swing. Still in the bulky dive suits, they tumbled to the ground, and an awful *thunk* made George go still. Augustus spit on the man. "Get up, you little weasel."

But George didn't move.

Luke ran to his side. A pool of red was underneath his friend's head. He put his face down to George's. There was no sound of breath. "George? George!"

Charlie rushed over as well, sending an accusatory glare to Augustus. "What have you done?"

Luke patted his friend's face. But his open eyes stared at. . . nothing.

Augustus stepped forward. "Let that be a lesson to both of you. Do *not* go against my wishes. Now get him out of the suit and clean up the mess. You'd better bury him too. Not a word or I'll follow through on my threats to your wives."

Luke lifted his chin and caught Charlie's eyes. What could they do now?

Augustus's footsteps sounded in the distance. He was just leaving them? To clean up his mess? The murder of their friend?

He dared to look over his shoulder at the man.

Rage built inside him.

The man had to be stopped.

Even if he had to risk his life to do it.

Margo
April 2, 1933

Hands on her shoulders made her fling her eyes open.

Luke was standing over her. His eyes were frantic. "You need to get up right now and pack. I am sorry, my love. But there is no other choice."

"I. . .I. . .don't understand." She rubbed the sleep from her eyes. "What happened?" Looking down at his hands, she gasped. "Is that blood?"

"Shhh." He sat down next to her. "I need you to be very quiet. And I need you to do exactly as I say. Please. Trust me."

Fully awake now, she grabbed onto his arm with both hands. "I will. But you have to tell me. What has put that fear in your eyes?"

His shoulders slumped. "I am sorry I did not tell you before. But a man named Augustus De Ville has threatened all of us. Made us dive and help him search for the gold. We did not lead him to it. And now George is dead." His voice cracked, and he pinched the bridge of his nose. "The man killed him tonight. Right in front of our eyes."

Her heart felt like it stopped for a moment and then raced to catch up. "What?!"

"Please. There is no time. Charlie and I have arranged for you and Amelia and the kids to go to Michigan. I cannot say anymore. A car will be here in a few minutes with them and will drive you to Colorado. From there you can take the train." He gave her an envelope. "Here. The tickets for everyone. But they are in different names, just to be safe. I do not wish anyone to find you."

It was all too much to take in. But seeing the frantic look in her husband's eyes made her come to terms with the truth that this was happening. It was real. Her heart clenched for her friend. "Does Amelia know about George?" Tears flooded her eyes.

"Yes. I just came from there. We had to take care of George's family for him."

He helped her to stand and grabbed a suitcase. "I will bring everything else later. Take only what you need. I am so sorry about the circumstances, but I could not bear it if anything happened to you." Crushing her to his chest, he kissed the top of her head. "Please. Go. Be safe."

"But what about you?" That awful man wouldn't kill Luke too, would he?

"I will finish the job that he expects and then leave. Charlie and I will figure out what to do. But we had to take care of you first."

Everything sunk in, and the gravity of the situation hit her full on. George had been killed. Oh, poor Amelia.

Margo moved around the room frantically, grabbing clothes and a few essential items. "I don't want to go without you."

"But you must." He glanced out the window. "The car is here. Please hurry."

A jolt brought her awake. The dark of night was still upon them. How far had they gone? Margo peered over her shoulder at Amelia and the children in the back seat. Tearstained cheeks all bore the same story. Loss. Pain. Hurt.

With barely more than the clothes on their backs, they were also leaving everything they'd ever known. In addition to losing husband and father. It wasn't right. *Oh God. How do we help them? How can we make this right?*

Turning her face back to the window beside her, she ran Luke's words to her over and over in her mind. He promised to write her every day. But she couldn't write back. At least not under her real name. He didn't want the man named Augustus De Ville to find them.

After they retrieved the rest of the gold for the man, they were devising a plan of how to escape before he killed them too. That was what worried Margo the most. After they'd done what he asked, what would keep him from murdering them? She'd suggested that maybe they run away before the last dive. But how?

There were too many variables.

Luke had stuffed gold nuggets into her suitcase under her clothes and told her to find a small place to live where she could help Amelia and the kids get through the horrendous loss of George. She didn't need to work for a while. It would be best to lie low.

Once Luke arrived, they could build a house and start over. It sounded like a beautiful plan. But what would they all have to endure until that time?

How had things gone so horribly wrong? She pressed a hand to her forehead. She wished he'd never seen the ship. Never found the gold.

But as a diver for the bridge, Luke still could have been hurt by this De Ville fellow. Especially if he needed help finding his treasure. What if it had been Luke instead of George? Her heart clenched at the thought, and tears clogged her throat.

Closing her eyes against the horrific thought, she realized what Amelia must be feeling. Probably only a tiny percentage of what the poor woman was going through, but Margo sat up a bit straighter and prayed for strength. Rather than living in fear and feeling sorry for herself and the circumstances, she could be a friend to Amelia and support her through this time.

God would see them through. *Yes, Lord, please.* She wasn't sure how, but she would put her faith in Him. One day soon, she'd see her husband again. She would. All of this would be behind them. It didn't matter if all of their dreams had been shattered. They had each other, and that was what mattered.

The Son

Killing that man before he had all his gold wasn't part of the plan. But at least the other two knew he was serious. Augustus had seen the fear in their eyes.

Fear helped people listen and do what they were told.

That's all he needed at this point. For them to listen to his instructions and carry them out.

It wouldn't take long now. They were motivated.

Things might be a bit riskier now, but it could easily be cleaned up. And he already had a plan for how to do it.

The French fellow could help him get his gold, and then all he had to do was disengage the guy's air hose and shove him into the hold of the ship. Once he was at the surface, he could take care of the other guy.

His father's legacy was being redeemed. He was worthy.

He would be rich.

Chapter 18

Flip
August 3, present day

Flip surveyed the crowd around him. His friend handed him the burner phone. "Untraceable. Toss it when you're done, and you're golden."

With a nod, he shoved it in his pocket, put on his dark sunglasses, and headed toward Pier 39. Even if they traced which cell towers the text pinged off, it would only lead to one of the busiest piers in the city.

With a few taps to the screen, he downloaded the picture he'd taken the other night to the burner.

Pulling up the hood on his sweatshirt, he kept his stride casual, looking like a tourist by stopping at shops along the way in the chilly morning air. He bought a few trinkets, a sandwich, and a coffee—all with cash. Then he went to one of the benches and began to eat his sandwich.

After several moments, he acted like he got a text. So he pulled out the burner and began to type:

MAYOR RILEY HIRED UNDERWATER ARCHAEOLOGIST KAYLA RICHARDSON TO BRING UP BURIED TREASURE NEAR THE GOLDEN GATE BRIDGE. SHE'S WORKING WITH STEVEN MICHAELS, WHOSE COMPANY IS UNDER INVESTIGATION FOR A BRIDGE COLLAPSE. WHAT ARE THEY UP TO? MS. RICHARDSON IS KNOWN FOR HER WORK, BUT WHERE IS THE MISSING ARTIFACT THAT WAS SUPPOSED to be given to the Smithsonian from the wreckage of the *Lily*? My sources say that she has it.

Ms. Richardson also said that she wouldn't dive without Mr. Michaels's help. But just two nights ago, she was seen alone, bringing up something from the wreckage. What is she hiding now? Is she stealing from the city? Are she and Mr. Michaels behind an elaborate plot to fleece the mayor?

You owe it to the citizens of San Francisco to uncover the truth. Corruption has no place here.

He attached the photo and sent it to every news outlet in town. The mayor's office would be flooded with calls. Even if no one ran with the story, the trap had been set. Mayor Riley couldn't allow Kayla to remain on the project now. At least not until the mess was cleared up. Which would probably take weeks.

Enough time for him to get down there and grab the gold.

He'd come up with a new plan last night. It required a lot of money for gear and extra tanks, but he could dive from beyond Alcatraz Island and use the DPVs to take him to the site underwater. He'd have to hire more guys, but that shouldn't be a problem. They could do it like they did in *The Italian Job*. Smuggle the gold out underwater. Granted, the waters were much more violent in the strait than in Venice, but he could take precautions.

In a matter of days, it would all be over.

Kayla

The buzzer sounded by her door. Padding across the carpet, she ran a hand through her hair. "Hello?"

"It's Steven." Just the sound of his voice made a shiver race up her spine.

"Come on up." It would be best to face it all head-on anyway.

She couldn't deny the fact that she cared for him. But he was probably furious with her for pushing him away. Trust and honesty were big things. Had she ruined it all by not trusting him—not believing in him?

A tap on the door.

She released the dead bolt and opened the door. "Hi."

"Hi." He had a gift bag in one hand and roses in the other. "These are for you."

Different emotions rushed her all at once and tangled in her brain. What was this? "I don't understand."

"This"—he offered her the bag—"is something I made for you. And these"—he held out the flowers—"are to show you that I care about you, Kayla Richardson. I need you to know that I am an honorable man. That I didn't do the things I've been accused of. And. . .I'm hoping that you will consider going out to dinner with me tonight."

Everything stopped. Staring into his eyes, she knew the truth. "Come on in." She took the flowers and bag and went to the kitchen. It had been way too long since anyone had given her roses. Didn't she have a vase? Somewhere?

With her hands on her hips, she looked at her kitchen cabinets and tried to picture where she would have put it.

"Can I help?" His voice was soft. Soothing. Three simple words, and it felt like little fingers of comfort wrapping around her heart.

"I can't remember where I put my vase."

He grimaced. "I'm sorry, I didn't think about that. I should have brought you one."

"No, it's around here somewhere. . ." She opened one cabinet, crouched down, and searched. "My dad used to bring me flowers." She wasn't sure why she told him that, but something about this guy always made her open up. "Wait! I think it's in the cabinet above the fridge." She stood up and closed the cupboard. When she looked up, she laughed. "So yes, I could use your help, because I can't reach it without a step stool."

The hesitance on his face disappeared. "It's good to hear you laugh. I was afraid I'd lost you."

"You didn't lose me." She stepped closer and put a hand on his arm. "I'm sorry for how I reacted, but it all took me by surprise."

"You were perfectly justified in that. I get it. A lot of information was thrown at you, and we didn't have enough history for you to know my integrity." He inched closer too.

Gazing up into his eyes, she studied him. Knew him. Understood him. Everything was clear. Right. With him, she was whole again. "I do know your integrity. I might not have had time to grasp it at the moment, but fear is an ugly beast in my life. Ever since my parents' deaths, I've struggled to find myself again. But then you came along. And it changed everything for me. You've done that, Steven. *You* found me. And I trust you with my whole heart. I do."

The smile that lifted the corners of his mouth touched her deep within. For a moment, she hoped that he would kiss her. Everything in her wanted that. But he turned to the fridge. "Let me get that vase."

Heat rushed through her as she went to trim the stems of the roses. "Thank you." The attraction she felt for this man was stronger than anything she'd ever felt.

He set the glass vase on the counter next to her and lifted up the bag again. "Aren't you going to open it?"

Out of the corner of her eye, she saw him wiggle his eyebrows. It made her giggle. She handed him the scissors. "Here, you take over, and I'll open it."

"What do I do?" A dumbfounded expression on his face, he blinked at her. His long lashes fanned his cheeks—why did God always give the best eyelashes to men? It wasn't fair.

Shaking her head of the thought, she showed him on the stem

where to cut. "Just trim each one of them an inch or two before we put them into water. It will help them last longer."

"Oh. . .okay." He went to work while she grabbed the bag.

It was the color of her living-room pillows. How thoughtful that he'd noticed her favorite color. When she peeked inside, the paper was the same, mixed with layers of white. Just like her color scheme. Man, the guy was observant.

Carefully pulling out the layers of tissue, she touched something smooth. Her breath caught in her throat. Tears stung her eyes. He'd *made* this for her? The thought made her want to sob right then and there in the kitchen. But she swallowed and tried to hide her emotion as she lifted the piece out.

It was even more beautiful as she brought it out. Two wooden dolphins—beautifully carved to look like they were jumping out of the water—were set on steel rods on a wooden base painted to match her living room. The finish was perfect and lacquered shiny and smooth. "I don't know what to say, Steven." She shook her head. "They're gorgeous."

"I'm glad you like them." The roses all in the vase, he moved closer to her again.

"Like them?" She sputtered for a moment, searching for words. "I love them. Thank you." She turned to him.

His gaze was soft. Tender. "I wanted to give you something special." He shrugged. "It was the best I could come up with. And it kept my hands busy."

"It's perfect." A tear slipped out of the corner of her eye.

He reached up and wiped it off her cheek. "I'm sorry. I didn't mean to make you cry."

"They're good tears. I promise." She pinched her lips together. "My Dad used to talk about making me some dolphins one day." She laughed at the memory. "He always said he wanted to be a carpenter like Jesus. But he had a friend at church teaching him and said that Dad was all thumbs. He came home with more Band-Aids on him each time than I ever had as a child growing up." She licked her lips. "Thank you. I can't tell you how much this means to me."

For several seconds, they stared into each other's eyes and the air around them seemed to be sucked out like in a vacuum. She didn't dare breathe.

He moved toward her, closing the space between them.

She still held the dolphins in her hands.

He leaned in and placed a gentle kiss on her lips. Sweet. With all the promise of tomorrow and the day after and the day after that. Then he pulled back and smiled.

No words passed between them for a few minutes as she went to the living room to place the dolphins by the windows. She tried to calm her racing heart.

As much as she'd felt in that simple kiss, she was thankful that he was a gentleman. Needed that desperately. Because she wasn't ready for all these feelings. Not yet.

He brought the roses into the room and stood beside her. They both stared out the window. "Would you like them in here?"

"Yes, please." She showed him where to place them and then had an idea. "Would you like to come with me to my lab?"

"Sure. Anything in particular we're going to work on?" They were back to familiar, comfortable ground.

"I've had a couple of my team working on the box."

"You found it and brought it up?"

"I did. And I'd really like to see what's inside it."

He drove them to her office, and they chatted about food. Of course. He'd reiterated his invitation to dinner that night, and she accepted. Another bright spot to look forward to.

When they reached the parking lot, she voiced the question she'd been wanting to ask all day. "Have you heard about the investigation? When they will be done?"

"I was told this morning that they would reveal their findings tomorrow. I'm sure it will be good news and we can get back to work."

"Good." Relief flowed through her limbs, and she let out a sigh. "I'm glad it's almost over."

"Me too. I hate that it happened in the first place, but one of my guys called last night and said that he wouldn't put it past one of our competitors to have been the anonymous source." The shake of his head as he turned off the engine made his sunglasses slide down his nose. He peered over the top of them. It was nice to see his eyes. "I hate that this is the world we live in—where you have to sabotage the competitor to get ahead—but I can only do the very best work that I can and stand tall on the fact that I've done the right thing. My integrity means a lot to me."

Reaching over, she grabbed his hand and squeezed. "It will be good to put all this behind you, I'm sure."

Her phone rang, and she looked at the caller ID. "It's the detective on my mom's case."

"Go ahead. I'm not in any hurry."

She swiped the screen to answer. "Hello?"

"Miss Richardson? This is Detective Collins. I've got some news. Do you have a moment?"

"Yes." It was a good thing she wasn't driving, because her hands began to shake.

Steven put his SUV into Park and waited.

"We found the owner of the vehicle. She died six months before the accident, and the car was being used by a grandson. But he was off at college and had left the vehicle at home in a barn because he was refurbishing it. The parents were in Europe on a river cruise.

Everything has been substantiated as to their whereabouts."

Her stomach plummeted. She cleared her throat. "What does that mean?"

The detective sighed. "It means that we don't have any answers. The keys were in the car in the barn. Anyone that knew it was there could have gone and taken it for a joyride. And without any forensic evidence, we have hit a dead end."

"So what you're telling me is that we'll never know who it was that killed my mother."

"Nothing is definitive, but the captain has declared that the case will not have any more resources put behind it. We can always reopen it later, but as of right now, we've exhausted every avenue that we could. I'm sorry." The tone of his voice was resigned.

"Thank you, Detective Collins. I appreciate all you've done."

"I'll call you if we come across anything else. Have a good day." He ended the call.

Putting the phone back in her pocket, she bit her bottom lip.

"I'm sorry, Kayla." This time Steven reached out and took her hand. But he held on. "I know this isn't easy."

She shared with him the details the detective had given her. "I have pushed for answers for so long. Tried to get to the truth because I just *had* to know. And now? I just feel numb. Maybe I *have* wasted too much time on this."

"I wouldn't call it a waste. Perhaps God has used this as part of the healing process?"

She turned to face him. "Always an optimist, I see."

"It's better than being a pessimist." He winked at her.

"I prefer the term *realist*."

He grinned and shook his head. "Why don't we go inside and get your mind off it. Let's see what your people have done with the box."

The lump in her throat only grew. But she nodded. "Okay." They unbuckled and got out of the car. He was right. She needed to get her mind off it.

When they entered her office, Carrie made a beeline for them. "We got it open." The girl bounced on her toes. "Just wait until you see this."

Kayla followed her, and they went into the lab area where tanks of water held many artifacts that they were trying to salvage and keep intact.

Carrie led them to the one with the box. They'd done a beautiful job of getting all the growth off it. It was open. "Look." She pointed to a glass bottle sitting outside the box.

Kayla and Steven stepped closer. The bottle had a note inside it.

Carrie lowered a robotic arm into the water. "Tell me when you want me to turn it."

"Okay." Kayla got as close to the tank as she could and began to read aloud:

This treasure within the Lucky Martha was discovered by Leopold De Ville on August 22, 1894. I hereby lay my claim to it.

"Turn it, please."
Carrie shifted the bottle.

If anyone dares to steal any of it, you will face the same fate as my friend here.

The bottle was still intact with its cork stopper, and the paper remained inside. They couldn't risk exposing it to air after the pressure it had been under for over a century. But what she wouldn't give to be able to examine the paper inside. "Who on earth was Leopold De Ville, and are we supposed to assume that he killed whoever it was that was wrapped in chains and buried there?"

Steven tilted his head back and forth. "The journal stated that the box had originally been in the hands of the skeleton, so it makes sense."

"Then the question is, Why didn't Leopold claim his treasure? He obviously had the equipment to dive down there in 1894. What kept him from getting it?"

"Maybe that's the next mystery we need to solve."

Her phone rang again. She groaned at the *Phantom* ringtone. "It's the mayor. Excuse me."

"Hello?"

"Kayla? We need to talk."

"All right."

"What exactly did you dive for two nights ago?"

Her face flushed. How did he know? "A box. I thought it might have a clue in it. We're looking at it right now, sir."

"I thought you weren't going to dive until we had cleared Mr. Michaels." Accusation filled the politician's voice.

"Um. . .well, yes, sir. But I wanted to see—"

"Miss Richardson. I'm tired of the games. Apparently, you and Mr. Michaels are colluding on some grand scheme to swindle the city. I won't stand for it. You're fired."

Chapter 19

Luke
April 4, 1933

Coming up out of the water, Luke signaled to Charlie to unhook him. A pod of whales had kept them from venturing to the ship earlier with Augustus. Thankfully, the man was scared of most fish and sea creatures, and the first time he came face-to-face with the giant mammal, he'd tugged on the rope to signal retreating to the surface. It had given them another night to figure out what to do. So he and Charlie had met back at the water at three in the morning.

They hurried in the dark to get everything put away and then made their way back to the locker room.

Once they were locked in and alone, Charlie spoke. "What did you find?"

Luke closed his eyes for a moment and took a long breath. "Augustus's father—at least I am assuming it is his father, since they bear the same last name—found the *Lucky Martha* and her treasure back in 1894. He murdered a man. The man we found in chains. He left a message in a bottle stating that if anyone stole his treasure, he would do the same to them."

"And the gold?"

"There is a lot of it down there. We cannot in good conscience allow this man to retrieve it. We cannot. Because he could do untold evils with it." Luke shook his head. "He has already murdered—who knows how many people. He is just like his father, it seems. But I do not know how to catch him. One thing is for certain. As soon as he is done with us, he will kill us. Just like George."

"We could run away. We have the gold we've already brought up. It's plenty." The fear in Charlie's face said it all. He was ready to run.

"But that does not solve the problem. Only puts others in danger once we are gone." He'd been praying and wracking his brain, but he still had no clear idea of how to deal with the bad man. "It seems we are stuck."

"Are we setting charges again tomorrow?"

"No. The high-pressure hoses will be used to clear the loose material from the bedrock. And I do not think he will wait any longer to reach the ship. His patience is nonexistent, and he knows we are running out of time."

Charlie looked resigned. "Well, I guess then. . .we will be back here later tonight."

"I am most sorry, Charlie. It is my fault you are involved with this."

The day flew by. Which was a good thing, because he'd had very little sleep and wouldn't have been able to make it if things had slowed down. But now he had to be ready. Alert. Augustus would be there any moment. Luke stretched and hoped Charlie would get here first. That way they could try to come up with a plan. Anything. He still didn't have any clear direction as to how to proceed, but he knew that the man needed to be put in jail for George's murder. He'd wanted to call the police immediately after it happened but realized he and Charlie would end up in jail. Not Augustus.

Before they went down tonight though, he was going to ask a question. Perhaps God could work through that.

Taking a seat on the iron beam they used to launch the swing, he sent a few more prayers to heaven.

"Luke." Charlie's steps behind him were slow and steady. "You doin' all right?"

"Tired. How about you, my friend?" He slapped his friend's back as he sat beside him.

"Same."

Heavy steps sounded behind them. So much for coming up with a plan. They hushed.

"Evening, gentlemen." Augustus's nasally voice drifted out to the ocean. "I see you're ready to go."

Luke stood up. "Yes. But you need to answer a question for me first."

"Oh? And what would that be?" The man got right up into his face.

"Are you related to Leopold De Ville?"

The man sneered. "How do you know that?"

"Because there is a note in a bottle down there, saying that he killed the man we found. Because it was his treasure."

Augustus's sneer turned to a smile. "See? I told you that treasure was mine. My pa found it."

"Then why didn't he bring it up?"

The man turned stiff and frowned. Grabbed Luke by the rim of the dive suit. " 'Cause he was killed. Thrown by his horse. But he was smart. Sent us a letter to tell us he'd found it. It's mine, and you can't try to say that it's not."

Luke held out his hands as if surrendering. "I was not trying to say that."

"Good." He let go and stepped back. "I'm tired of all this waiting. Murky water, whales, and everything else. We are getting my gold tonight."

"It may take many trips. The weight alone will tax the hoist."

Augustus's nostrils flared, and he stuck his finger in Luke's chest. "I don't care how many trips it takes. We are getting that gold."

Luke nodded and looked at Charlie. They needed some sort of miracle, but so far God hadn't given him any kind of clue.

Once their helmets were in place, Charlie connected the air hoses and made sure everything was functioning properly.

Luke and Augustus climbed onto the swing and were plunged into the water.

It was a good thing they couldn't talk, because Luke would hate to have to try and converse with the awful man.

But as his thoughts turned darker toward Augustus, he felt convicted in his heart.

Jesus died for all. And that included Augustus.

No, God. No. I do not want to think of him as redeemable. He killed my friend!

But the pressing on his heart didn't stop. He closed his eyes and fought the feeling that he had to repent and show the love of Christ to the man beside him. But how could he do that when he'd witnessed the man take another life?

The war within him raged as they reached the seafloor.

Augustus pushed him forward, and Luke knew that he was expected to find the ship. And quick.

At least the water was a bit clearer. But the current was strong and churned the water. At times he couldn't see, so he'd have to rely on what he could feel and try to head in the correct direction.

Twenty minutes later, he found the stakes and lowered himself over the edge of the underwater cliff. As much as he didn't want Augustus to get the gold, Luke felt relieved. At least they could tie off a rope onto something so that on the other trips down, they could simply follow the rope as a guide and find it again.

A long night stretched before him. Perhaps by the end, God would give him the wisdom in how to handle the situation. Maybe if he turned himself in to the police and he and Charlie told the truth about all that happened, they could get Augustus arrested.

It might be worth a shot. But if he went to jail, what would happen to Margo?

They worked themselves into the inside of the sunken ship, and Luke opened the hatch they'd worked loose. Augustus pushed his way in to get a closer look and immediately started filling the net at his side. He motioned Luke closer, but Luke pretended not to see him. He went over to another area of the ship and looked around. He didn't want to help this man, so he was going to make it as hard as possible.

But then he spotted another seam that looked like it could be another hatch. Quickly turning his head so his light wouldn't give anything away to Augustus, he accidentally rammed his head into Augustus's helmet.

The man was furious. That much was clear. He pushed Luke and then grabbed him and made harsh motions to the net at Luke's side and pointed to the other hatch. Then he shook Luke. Hard.

Out of instinct, Luke pushed back. Which only made the man angrier.

Augustus went for his helmet.

No! He would die if he unlatched it or, worse, opened the front window.

But fighting underwater was a difficult thing. No moves could be done in a fast motion, and he couldn't get away from Augustus. So he pushed with all his might.

Augustus floated toward the hold, and Luke took the chance to try and make it out to the swing. The man's temper had taken over, and he didn't want to be the next victim.

But as he swam out of the ship, Augustus grabbed his leg.

Luke tugged on the hull of the ship to try and get leverage, but Augustus pulled back.

He tried to kick with his legs, but his opponent was strong.

With every ounce of his strength, he pulled with his arms and used both feet to try and push off of Augustus. It worked, and Luke's suit scraped the outside of the ship as he swam through the opening.

A flurry of bubbles followed him.

That could only mean one thing. He turned around and watched in horror as Augustus drowned inside his suit. Their fight had somehow dislodged the air hose.

Panic filled him. Had he just killed a man?

He shivered, and bile rose up his throat. He couldn't vomit in the suit. He wouldn't.

Swimming away from the ship as fast as he could, he untied the rope and went to the swing and yanked for all he was worth to get Charlie to bring him to the surface.

Margo
April 4, 1933
Lake Michigan

Sleep wouldn't come. Not tonight. Probably not for many nights.

She'd arrived in Michigan with Amelia and the children. But as soon as they found a place to stay and walked in the door, Amelia fell apart.

It was understandable. The woman had lost her husband and then been forced to leave everything she knew in the middle of the night and race across the country, hoping they wouldn't be found.

The children were grieving. Amelia was grieving. And Margo was trying to keep them alive. She'd prayed for strength over and over across the miles. Now her heart ached for Luke in a way she couldn't fathom. Fear and doubt tried to overcome her.

Margo got up from her bed and padded toward the kitchen.

She hadn't had a chance to buy any groceries yet, but maybe a cool glass of water would help.

If only it could wash away all the loss.

She filled a glass with water from the tap and sat at the little table. Luke had given her specific instructions about cashing in the gold, and she'd followed them to the letter. The president of the bank had assured her that her transaction was confidential. She even had a stamped and signed document to prove it.

It was amazing what money could do. They'd found a nice little house on the lake. It felt comforting. Serene. Safe.

But she had to protect them. Somehow.

How she longed to hear Luke's voice.

Margo. She could hear him breathing her name against her hair. Just like he had on their wedding night.

Her breath caught in her throat. She closed her eyes and imagined him saying her name again.

But then her heart thudded. An urgency flooded her. Pressed in on her.

Without another thought, she got down on her knees. Something was happening. And she needed to pray.

Right now.

Chapter 20

Kayla
August 4, present day

Pacing her small living room, she sipped on a cup of hot cocoa. After the mayor had fired her, she sent everyone home and locked up her offices. Fine. She'd been accused of something she didn't do.

Just like Steven.

What a coincidence.

She shook off the sarcastic thoughts. But it was true. Why couldn't everyone else see that they were being set up?

After Steven saw her home, he told her that he wanted to talk to his guys. Someone had to know something, and he wanted to get to the bottom of it.

Men. They always tried to fix things. But how was that any different than what she'd tried to do about her mother's case all this time? She understood why he wanted to do it.

For some reason, she only felt relief.

Relieved to have some time alone. Everything about this assignment had exhausted her. And frankly, she didn't have any fight left in her. The fact that Steven wanted to fight her battle was fine with her. At least for today. Tomorrow she might feel differently, but that was tomorrow.

She set down her cup on the coffee table and sat on the floor, crossing her legs like she had as a child. Maybe if she read Luke's journal again, she could find another clue. The thought that he might be one of the men buried with the ship made her heart ache. She'd gotten attached to the French diver who wanted to make a new life in America and raise a family.

After rereading the entire thing, her legs were cramping, and she stretched them out in front of her. Nothing else made sense. Luke must have died.

The buzzer sounded, and she stood up, her feet and legs shooting pins and needles. As she crossed the carpet, she checked her watch. Had she really been sitting there for more than three hours?

She pushed the talk button on the buzzer. "Who is it?"

"It's me." Steven's voice crackled in the speaker. "I have a surprise."

"Come on up. I love surprises." Just what she needed. Something to make her smile. Hopefully it had absolutely nothing to do with the whole *Lucky Martha* project.

As she opened the door, she caught sight of Steven helping a lovely gray-haired woman up the stairs. Who was this?

Steven saw her and smiled. Then he walked the woman to the door. "Kayla Richardson, may I introduce you to Lilian Taylor."

"It's nice to meet you. Please, come in." As the older woman passed, Kayla gave an inquiring look to Steven. What was he up to?

"Thank you for having me. It's been a long day of travel."

"Oh?" Kayla motioned to the couch. "Make yourself comfortable. Can I get you a glass of water or anything?"

"Water would be lovely, thank you."

She went to the kitchen to get a glass of water and came back to find Steven chatting freely with the woman as if they were old friends. "So how long have you known each other?" Why did she feel like she was in a game of twenty questions?

"We just met." Lilian smiled. "He's such a nice man." She patted his face.

Kayla raised her brows. "I must admit, now I'm even more curious."

Steven's face broke into a wide grin. "As much as I'd like to keep you guessing, I'll let Lilian tell you her story. She's traveled all the way from Michigan."

"Michigan?" That state had been on her mind a lot lately as she wondered about Margo.

The lovely older woman took a long sip, and her eyes sparkled as she turned to face her. "I brought something for you."

She put a hand to her chest. "For me? But why?"

Lilian reached down into her bag and pulled out a book. It was old and worn. She handed it to Kayla.

Opening the front cover, a gorgeous sketch drew her in. As she turned the page, more sketches filled page after page.

"This was my grandmother's."

Breathing out the name, Kayla could barely believe it. "Margo?"

"Yes." Lilian turned back to Steven. "My granddaughter loves to be on her phone, you see. All the time she's scrolling and posting and tweeting and whatever else all you young people do nowadays. Anyway, she saw something online about how this young man was looking for a woman name Margo Moreau. She messaged the contact, and he called me last night. And here I am."

"Margo was your grandmother? That is such a relief. We were so worried about what happened to her."

"But wait." Steven looked like he could barely contain himself. "There's more."

"I'm not buying something off of an infomercial, am I?" Kayla laughed and looked back and forth between the two.

"No." Lilian pulled something else out of her bag. "But I do think you'll want to read this." She handed over several yellowed pages. "Luke and Margo were my grandparents."

"He lived?"

"Yes. In fact, he lived a very long life." She patted the papers. "Why don't you read this, and then I'll answer any questions you have. I have quite a few myself, but I'll wait until you have a chance to read."

"Okay." Kayla opened the pages and recognized the same loopy script she'd seen in the journal. Except this time it was in English. Written by Luke.

I have lived a long and happy life. The Lord has indeed blessed. But before I die, there is something that plagues me that I must confess. I want my beautiful family to know a burden that I have carried. It has been my greatest joy to be your father, grandfather, and now great-grandfather. But I am in no way perfect.

Many years ago, back in 1933, I had a job as a diver working on construction of the Golden Gate Bridge. It was during my work that I discovered a ship buried in the strait. A ship that held gold.

While I had a journal long ago that detailed the whole story, it is surely lost, and I do not wish to retell it all. But what happened at the end is what brought us to Michigan.

To be honest, in my desperation to gain money, I put everyone I cared about in danger. Margo was threatened. And a very bad man killed my friend George. All because of that gold. Because of greed.

I sent Margo away to the only living relative she had in Michigan, and I stayed, helping this man. But one night, down in the depths of the boat, we fought. His air hose was knocked loose, and he drowned.

I am responsible for that man's death. And for that I am most sorry. Please forgive me.

I am nothing more than a sinner, but bountifully saved by grace. I know that God sees me as forgiven and clean because of what Christ did on the cross, but I have always regretted not sharing the Gospel with that man before he died. No matter what he did to George or to me or to anyone else. I had the opportunity, and I did not do it.

Don't waste your time mourning me once I am gone. But please, share the Good News with everyone. Even those who have wronged you. Even those who you think are evil and beyond forgiveness.

That is the legacy I wish to leave. A legacy of God's love to all.

Yours lovingly,
Luke Moreau

Kayla laid the papers in her lap and shook her head. "I am so thrilled to hear that he lived, but now I'm even more puzzled. Who is it that is buried with the ship?" She pointed the question to Steven.

He shook his head. "I don't know. But it wasn't Luke."

Lilian lifted a finger. "It was Augustus De Ville. After Grandpa wrote that letter, he told Grandma everything the last few days of his life. The day after Augustus drowned, Grandpa dove back down to get the suit off of Augustus so it wasn't missing for work. They'd pulled the hose up the night before, and he and Charlie were so shocked and upset that they decided to come back early the next day. Grandpa left Augustus there and then filled in the ship with as much mud as he could. He said he hoped that it would never be found again."

"He didn't try to get any more of the gold?"

"No." Lilian gave her a sad smile. "As you now know, they had some. Grandpa built a home for Grandma Margo and built one for Amelia and her family next door. And they provided for her and the kids until she married again. I grew up with Great-Aunt Amelia in my life. Oh, the stories she and Grandma could tell."

Incredible. Kayla's heart felt lighter knowing that there was at least a happy ending for Luke and Margo. But what a weight they must have carried all those years.

Kayla picked up the leather journal. "This is in French. But perhaps you would like to have it. After all, it belongs to your family. I have the translation here so you can read it and know more of his story."

"I would love to. Thank you." Lilian reached out and took the book. Running a hand over the top, she stared at it for several moments, and Kayla saw a tear slip down her cheek.

She waited for Lilian to look up. "I think it's wonderful that you came all the way out here to help solve our mystery about Margo, but you could have just told us on the phone."

"True." Lilian tilted her head. "But then I wouldn't have the excuse to fulfill my grandpa's last wish."

Steven tilted his head. "What was that?"

"That one of his family members would go see the completed Golden Gate Bridge in person and walk across it since he never had the chance to do so."

The request made Kayla tear up as she shared a glance with

Steven. "I would be honored if we could accompany you tomorrow, Miss Taylor."

"I would love that. Thank you."

Maybe some good came out of this project after all.

Steven

August 5

The Golden Gate Bridge was a massive structure that struck awe in Steven as he waited at the parking lot on the southeast. He and Kayla stood off to the side to give Lilian a moment to take it all in. As soon as they'd exited the car, tears had glistened in the woman's eyes, and she put both hands over her mouth.

Several minutes later, she pointed to the south tower. "That is where my grandfather dove and worked?"

Kayla stepped closer to Lilian and put a hand on the woman's shoulder. "Yes. Your grandfather was key. This bridge wouldn't be here today without his work."

The older woman nodded and shook her head. "It's so big."

The heavy breeze whisked around them, and Steven shoved his hands into his pockets. Words weren't necessary at the moment.

Amazing how he'd driven across the bridge hundreds of times, but his perspective changed as he stood here with it looming before him. And now that he understood even more what it took to build it almost ninety years ago, his respect and reverence for the men who accomplished the feat grew.

He stepped up to Lilian and offered his arm. "Are you ready?"

She took a deep breath, and her shoulders rose. "Yes. Let's walk across." She wrapped her heavy sweater around her tighter. The weather was cool and pleasant, but the wind made it downright chilly over the water.

Taking slow steps so the older woman had time to savor each

moment, Steven escorted Luke's granddaughter over the walkway.

Kayla talked about the history of the bridge and what Luke's job entailed. After about ten minutes, they stopped and stood at the side, looking at the water.

Lilian shivered beside him. "I can't imagine what it must be like to be under that water. And so deep too." She shook her head. "The stories Grandpa told always had us on the edge of our seats as children, but we couldn't imagine it. We'd pretend to dive in the bathtub or out at the lake, but a few inches of water is nothing compared to this. Over time, we all got busy with life. I'm sad that none of the family came here before."

Steven squeezed Lilian's hand that was in the crook of his arm. "But you're here now. That's what matters."

The next two hours they spent walking casually along the bridge, stopping here and there for Lilian to talk about her family and ask questions, and for Steven and Kayla to share whatever information they had.

"Would you tell me about the ship? Grandpa wouldn't ever speak about it, but our grandma did. Every once in a while. She'd rave about how brave our grandfather was and how he provided for our family."

They stopped in the middle of the bridge and looked back at the south tower. Kayla began with the history of the ship and the legends that came out of the gold rush. Steven watched her face light up. Her hands moved as she spoke, and Lilian was just as caught up in the story as she was.

Listening to Kayla's passion as she talked about the *Lucky Martha*, Steven entertained the idea of working on more underwater archaeology digs. Especially if it gave him the opportunity to spend more time with Miss Richardson.

The thought made him smile.

"You love all this history too, don't you, Mr. Michaels?" Lilian had turned back to him.

"I have to admit I do. The artifacts we brought up from the ship are fascinating."

She turned back to Kayla. "Do you think I could see them?"

Kayla's sweet smile made her blue eyes shine. "Of course. Would you like to go there now?"

"Oh yes." Lilian placed her hand back in the crook of Steven's arm. "Thank you both for doing this for me."

"It's our pleasure." Steven returned her smile and looked over the older woman's head to Kayla. The emotion in her face said it all. This was why she did what she did.

An hour later, they'd walked back to the car and had driven over to Kayla's office and lab. Kayla had told Lilian all about the box. The box that Luke had found too.

Lilian's excitement had grown. She couldn't wait to see and touch something that her grandfather had found underwater in 1933.

Kayla went to the door with her key and gasped. "Steven. Look."

He left Lilian's side and saw the door ajar. He pushed Kayla behind him. "What about the security system?"

"It's not blaring, and I never got a call, so someone must have disarmed it. . .but I don't know how." Kayla's voice was a bit shaky.

"Call the police. You two stay out here, and I'll check it out. Everything seems quiet, so maybe they're gone." Steven inched the door open and surveyed the front room. Not a sign of anyone. The place wasn't ransacked. What had they been after?

When he turned and looked at the alarm panel, it had been ripped off the wall with wires rerouted to a battery on the floor. What on earth?

But everything was quiet. Whoever they were, they must have come and gone. He checked the lab and the other rooms. Nothing.

Steven went back out to the foyer and looked at Kayla. "There's no one here."

She and Lilian walked into the offices. Kayla looked around. "I can't see anything out of place. But we'd better go check the lab."

She led the way into the large room that held all the artifacts they'd been working on. Kayla put a hand to her chest and let out a big breath. "Good. They didn't destroy any of the equipment."

"Is everything here?" Steven walked to the tanks on the other side of the room and peered into them.

"I don't know. I'll need to check each one."

Lilian gasped from the doorway.

Steven turned. "Danny! What are you doing?"

His friend held a knife to the older woman's throat. "Not another step, Steven." He lifted his chin. "Now this is what we're going to do. Kayla, you're going to pack up every artifact in here from the *Lucky Martha*. And I know you've got some of the gold nuggets here too."

Kayla crossed her arms over her chest. "It was you, wasn't it? That sabotaged the equipment? You can't get away with this, Danny. We *know* you. What. . .are you going to kill all of us?"

"Maybe." His face had turned hard.

Steven stepped closer to Kayla.

"Nuh-uh." Danny brought the knife closer, and Lilian whimpered. "Not another step, Steven. But you can help pack up things. We wouldn't want anything to happen to Mrs. Taylor, now would we?"

An ocean wave of emotion rolled over Steven. He'd trusted this guy. Vouched for him. Worked with him for years. "No need for threats, Danny. We'll do what you ask." Prayerfully, the police would come soon.

"Always the guy in charge, aren't you, Steven? Well, not this time. Start packing." He kicked a stack of tubs toward them.

It took about ten minutes to pack all the items in the tubs. The entire time, he'd avoided looking at Kayla because his heart couldn't take it. He didn't want Danny to think they were trying to communicate in any way. The best thing to do was go along with Danny's instructions and keep everyone safe. But as soon as they were done, Steven was at a loss. What next? How could he protect Kayla and Lilian?

A huge guy appeared at the door. He was about the same height as Steven but looked like a bodybuilder. He went up to Danny and tipped his chin at him. "Hey, Flip, just heard from the crew. We're ready to go."

A sneer crossed Danny's face. "Good. We'll just take these three with us. . .just in case we need insurance to get away."

The big man pulled out a gun and pointed it at Kayla. "Let's go."

Chapter 21

Margo
May 28, 1937
Lake Michigan

The sandy beach of Lake Michigan stretched in front of her. The Lord had truly blessed them. They had a beautiful home, Luke had a good job, Amelia and the children were next door, and their Father in heaven had blessed them with two beautiful babies.

Simone and Matthew played in the sand beside her, their chubby little arms flinging their plastic shovels this way and that.

Pulling her sketch pad into her lap, Margo wanted to capture this moment—they wouldn't be babies much longer. Oh, they grew so fast.

"Good morning, my love." Luke's voice from behind her made her turn.

"Good morning."

He took off his shoes in the grass and walked barefoot across the sand to her.

Luke placed a kiss on her forehead as he knelt down beside her. "The bridge was opened yesterday for people to walk across." He held out a newspaper with a black-and-white picture on the front page. The bridge was incredible.

Her breath caught in her throat. "Gracious, it's magnificent, isn't it?"

He nodded and looked out at the water. But his smile didn't reach his eyes.

"What is it?"

Luke settled next to her and wrapped his arm around her shoulders. Letting out a shaky breath, he reached up with his other hand to swipe away a tear. "I have often wondered why the Lord allowed me to survive."

"You're thinking of George." Her heart ached for her husband. Many a night he awoke, covered in sweat after a nightmare about what had happened.

"Yes. He was a good friend. The very best."

"It wasn't your fault, Luke."

He tilted his head to the side. "I have gone over the events hundreds of times in my brain. I know the good Lord has forgiven me for my part in it, and He saw to bless us through it all, even with my failures. But the what-ifs still plague me. I wonder if there was anything else I could have done. And what it would be like to have my friend here with me today."

Her mouth went dry. Would he always carry the burden? The guilt? *Oh Lord, please help him. Show me how I can encourage him through this time.*

He lifted the paper again and stared at it. "It is the longest suspension bridge in the world. And I am indeed proud of the fact that I had the privilege to work on its construction. But I wish that George and I could have seen it finished."

"Maybe someday we can go back and walk across it ourselves."

He turned to her, and his face relaxed. "I would love that. Thank you, my love." He placed a long, sweet kiss on her lips. "Perhaps after the summer work is done? If I remember correctly, September and October in San Francisco are quite lovely."

"Well. . ." She sent him a coy grin. "Maybe *next* summer."

"Oh?" His eyebrows raised.

"I'm not sure I should be traveling then."

A new light shone in his eyes. "Tell me."

"I was waiting for the perfect moment to let you know. . .but we are expecting another baby. Beginning of December if my calculations are correct!"

"Oh Margo! That is the best news." He pulled her close.

She whispered against his ear. "And if it's a boy, I think we should name him George."

He pulled back a few inches and placed his forehead against hers. "It is perfect."

Chapter 22

Kayla
August 5, present day

"Put your hands behind your back." Danny sent his hulking friend over to zip-tie their hands. "Everyone will be fine if you just cooperate."

Lilian's eyes were wide. Would the older woman be able to handle the stress?

"Why don't you let Mrs. Taylor go. You could lock her in my back office and just take us." Kayla pleaded with Danny.

"Nah, I think it's better this way. You two will behave better if you're worried about the old lady." The smirk that covered Danny's face infuriated her. But what could she do? She thought of everything in her office. Was there any way to get an advantage?

Steven stood straighter even as the big guy cinched the zip ties tighter. "We won't cause any trouble, Danny. Just let Mrs. Taylor go."

"Stop, right where you are! Put down your weapons!" Voices shouted from the door.

Kayla's eyes went wide as Steven rammed himself into the big guy behind him and his gun slid across the floor.

By the time she looked back at Danny, the sheriff had him in cuffs and an officer was seeing to Lilian.

The whole thing was over in what seemed like a split second.

Steven was beside her. "You okay?"

"Yeah. At least I think so." Her heart raced in her chest.

An officer cut the ties off her wrists. She rubbed at them and took a few deep breaths. It was over.

Steven

August 6, present day

The mayor's conference room was packed with members of the press. It was bright and sunny with the scent of fresh-brewed coffee in the air. Steven had finally slept a full eight hours last night. For the first time in a while.

The air around him practically buzzed. Everyone was eager to hear about the incredible story the mayor himself had promised them. Steven sat near the back and sent a prayer up for Kayla and her part of today. She hadn't been looking forward to it. But soon things could get back to normal. They could get back down to the ship and finish what they had started. Eventually it would be nice to put the whole thing behind them.

Lilian walked in the room and spotted him.

He waved her over.

"I saved you a seat."

"Thank you." Her smile was wide. "I must say, this isn't exactly how I envisioned my trip out here, but it has definitely been an adventure."

The mayor and his entourage entered the room.

Steven sent Lilian a smile and turned back to the front. When Kayla entered, a deep sense of pride filled him. This woman was amazing.

"Good morning." Mayor Riley stepped to the microphone. The crowd hushed. The mayor asked for everyone to take a seat. "Thank you all for coming on such short notice. Before we get to the real reason I called you all here today, I need to inform you that every paper and news outlet here today needs to run a retraction of their stories on Mr. Steven Michaels and Miss Kayla Richardson. The allegations against both were untrue. You were fed false information from the man behind the criminal activity. Mr. Danny Pool is in the sheriff's custody, and the sheriff's office will be sending the proof and correction for the story today." He nodded to the sheriff. "The DA will be prosecuting Mr. Pool. Sheriff." He stepped back.

The sheriff stepped forward. "When we searched Mr. Pool's apartment, we found all the evidence we needed—"

"What was all this about?" The interruption came from a woman in the front row who voiced the question surely on everyone's mind.

The mayor moved back to the podium. His grin wide. "While doing restoration on the base of the south tower, Mr. Michaels and his team stumbled upon a find of great significance for our city: the *Lucky Martha*."

The room erupted in chatter and questions. But the mayor held up his hands to silence them all. "Please. Reserve all of your questions for the end. We will get to them." The mayor turned to Kayla. "Miss Richardson?"

She stepped to the podium with her notes in her hand. Her hair was down, and she looked relaxed. "Thank you, Mr. Mayor. I am Kayla Richardson, the archaeologist hired by the city to recover what we could out of the *Lucky Martha*. I'm sure most of you know the legend that surrounded the ship. But what you may not be aware of is the topography of the seafloor in the strait and how difficult it is to dive in those waters. While I won't go into detail now, I will gladly send your offices details if you'd like. Because of the challenges the water and tides present, the ship has remained—fairly intact—buried in the seawall, just beyond the south tower where the floor then drops pretty substantially. The depth of the strait at the base of the tower is around 110 feet. But beyond that, the depth grows to more than 300 feet. It's in the cliff wall at the drop-off point that the ship has been buried over time."

She took a breath and looked down at her notes. "On our first dive down to the ship, we discovered human remains. The medical examiner informed us that we were dealing with two bodies that had been buried with the ship during two different eras. One sometime in the 1890s. The other around 1933 when construction on the bridge began. We found this interesting since the ship was said to have sunk back in 1849. After more examination, we have discovered the mystery around the *Lucky Martha* was multigenerational and multifaceted."

Several hands raised, but Kayla shook her head and continued. "Mr. Danny Pool was in possession of a journal written by Augustus De Ville and some items from Augustus's father, Leopold De Ville, as well. The journal also contained a letter from Leopold. We are pretty certain that Leopold is responsible for the death of a man who was wrapped in chains and drowned in the ship.

"Apparently Leopold made his living stealing other people's treasure finds. That is, until his wife left him and took their son, Augustus, to live on the other side of the country. This pushed Leopold into killing a man to steal his diving apparatus. The plan was to take his little team of criminals and find gold themselves. From all the tall tales he'd heard, there were several sunken ships around the peninsula that, according to legends, held berths of gold. He thought he and a few of his criminal friends could find all the gold that must be surrounding the peninsula." She licked her index finger and flipped to the next page.

"Leopold apparently found the *Lucky Martha* and sent a letter to his wife stating that they were going to be rich, and he was coming for her and his son. But before he could bring the gold to the surface, he had an accident one day in which his horse threw him and killed him. It wasn't until Augustus went searching for information about his father that he found the landlady Leopold had rented from. After his death, she had boxed up the few things that she thought were of value. Augustus acquired them and wanted to believe that his father had fully intended to return to him and his mother. His journal is full of angst about the father he never knew. But then the beginning of construction on the south tower messed everything up for him. He couldn't acquire the gold because one of the divers working on the bridge had already found it. Eventually, he threatened many of the divers and tried to use them to get the gold out of the ship. But he died in the ship when his air hose came undone. That accounts for the other bones we found.

"When Mr. Pool came into possession of the journal and letter from the De Villes, he put his own plan into action to retrieve the treasure. But once again, the bridge stood in the way of the criminals. Mr. Michaels stumbled upon the ship and reported it to the city immediately, knowing that they would need experts to handle the historical artifacts. Over time, we discovered that Mr. Luke Moreau was one of the divers who worked on the construction of the bridge. He also found the ship. His granddaughter is with us today. It is through Mr. Moreau's journals, his wife's sketches, and the journals from Augustus De Ville that we have been able to piece together the mystery that has surrounded this ship for more than 170 years. While greed pushed Leopold and Augustus to commit horrible acts, my team is pleased to be working on the recovery of a find of such historical significance for the city of San Francisco."

Kayla stepped back as the mayor stepped forward.

Hands were raised all over the room. Mayor Riley pointed to one. "Yes?"

"Is the legend true? About the gold?"

"Yes." He looked proud as a peacock. "This is a proud day for San Francisco." He pointed to another. "Sally?"

"What are the charges against Mr. Pool?"

He cleared his throat. "The list is long. My press secretary will be sending a press release with all the pertinent information shortly."

The mayor raised his eyebrows. "Mark, go ahead."

"How many people were murdered over the treasure?"

Steven shook his head. Of course, the reporters would want to know that.

Mayor Riley frowned. "We know of two for sure, but there is evidence to show that there were more. This is a good chance for us to be thankful and remember all the men who bravely worked on the building of the Golden Gate Bridge."

Lilian leaned closer to Steven and whispered. "It amazes me what men will do for gold. My own grandpa said it was easy to see how men got caught up in the gold rush because it's allure was so strong. But after he saw the devastation it caused, he wanted to get as far away from it as he could."

After reading through Luke's journal a couple of times, Steven had often tried to put himself in the man's shoes. Luke seemed to have a strong faith, but the Depression was difficult. To come face-to-face with a fortune would have tested any man's integrity. It made Steven wonder what he would have done given the same circumstances.

The questions continued for another half hour until the mayor told everyone that they would be receiving the press release and he would gladly hold another press conference once the project was completed.

For now, the news outlets had plenty of information for sensational stories to grace their pages and headline their newscasts.

Steven stayed in his seat and watched Kayla leave with the mayor's entourage. At least this part was over and they'd be able to get back to the part she loved. Underwater.

The room emptied of all the press. And Kayla came back in. She relaxed her shoulders as she approached. "Whew. At least that's over."

Lilian stood. "I think I'm going to get a cup of coffee. Would either of you like one?"

"I'd love one. Thank you." Steven sent the older woman a smile.

Kayla plopped down into the seat next to him. "So. . .what now?"

"My offer still stands to help you recover what you need from the ship."

"I was hoping you'd say that." She reached back and twisted her hair into a knot and stabbed it with a pen. "It's going to take a lot of work."

"I don't mind. I'm not going anywhere."

"Good." She looked up at him, and her stomach growled.

He laughed with her. "I'll take that as my cue." He stood up. "Kayla, would you like to have dinner with me?"

She narrowed her gaze. "You mean. . .like a date?"

He nodded. "Exactly."

"I'd love to."

Chapter 23

Kayla
Six months later
February 5, present day

The comfortable couch engulfed her as she sat next to Steven, his arm around her shoulders.

Their pastor and his wife sat across from them.

Jeremy smiled. "So have you set a date?"

Steven looked at her. "We're thinking July."

Her heart overflowed as she nodded.

"Good. That gives us plenty of time to do the premarital counseling." Jeremy leaned forward and put his elbows on his knees. "Kayla, how are you doing now that the big project is over?"

"It was a challenging job." Thinking back over the last few months, she couldn't believe all that it had entailed. Hundreds of dives. All the artifacts to clean and catalog. And then there was all the gold. A massive treasure. "I'm thankful that we're done."

"Have you taken some time off?" The pastor raised an eyebrow.

"Yes. Steven and his company had to get back to work on the bridge, so it was good for me to take some time. I went back to visit Mom and Dad's graves. Did a lot of crying. Even went to see my counselor, Johnathon, a few more times."

"And?"

Steven squeezed her shoulder.

She took a deep breath. "I admitted that I had been obsessed with finding who killed my mother. Johnathon had been urging me to let it go. And you know, I might have assumed that I had to let it go so that God would then give me the answer. But I've realized I have to be content *not* knowing. God is not obligated to give me an answer. When I told Johnathon that, he just about fell off his chair. But then he congratulated me on working through it. Even told my superiors that I was cleared until the next six-month check."

"That's great. Any more nightmares?" Jeremy's tone was soft.

"No. Not for several months now."

"That's fantastic." The man smiled as he grabbed his wife's hand. "It sounds like you two are ready for this next step."

She turned and looked into Steven's eyes. "I am."

"Me too." Steven mouthed, *I love you.*

A little chill raced up her spine. Oh, how she loved this man. It was amazing to her how they'd connected so perfectly. God's fingerprints were all over it.

He'd brought Steven into her life at just the right time. And He'd brought growth to them both through it all. "I love you," she whispered back to him. "Always."

Acknowledgments

Katia Rougeau Pena: What would I have done without you? I love you dearly and am so thankful that you were one of my very first "kids" twenty-six-plus years ago. Having you in my life has been such a joy, and your expertise on San Francisco after your umpteen years of living there was priceless to this story. Thank you! I can't wait to see you in person again so that I can hug your neck and love on those sweet babies of yours. Let's take another trip to the bridge. I'm even more fascinated with it now.

My critters Darcie Gudger, Becca Whitham, Kayla Woodhouse Whitham, Jana Riediger: Gracious, I am not whole without you guys. Becca and Kayla: You two saved my bacon on this story. Thank you again. Seriously.

And my brainstorming buddies, Jaime Jo Wright, Tracie Peterson, and Cheryl Hodde (along with Becca, Darcie, and Kayla above): This book would not be in the readers' hands without you guys. I love all of you so very much. Jaime, thank you for giving me your much-needed expertise. Love you!

Becca Weidel and Renette Steele: You lovingly did word wars with me at the end and helped me make it through.

Jeremy, my amazing hubby who is my best friend and biggest supporter: Even though you say you're not a "creative person," you sure do come up with some great ideas, and you always tell me I can do it—even when it feels like I need to write an entire book in a week. Your smile always lifts my spirits, and I love getting to share life with you. We have had one adventure after another, and I'm looking forward to even more ahead. Thank you for loving me—flaws and all.

Becky Fish: Working with you is always such a joy! If I'm remembering correctly, five of the books you've edited for me with Barbour have won awards or been in the finals. That is in huge part due to your expertise. Thank you for working with my craziness once again.

The team at Barbour: Once again it has been great to work with you on another project. Becky Germany, you are a treasure. Laura Young, you're always happy to help with my questions and work with me. Abbey Warschauer, thank you for all the work on the website for the Doors to the Past series. And thank you to all the rest of the team!

My advisory board and prayer partners: Karen Ball, Martha Ilgenfritz, Amanda Schmitt, Jeni Koch, Darcie Gudger, Kayla Whitham, Tracie Peterson, Jackie Hale, Christi Campbell, Sheryl Farnsworth—thank you all so very much.

To God be the glory.

Thank you for joining me for another story. God bless you all.

Consider it pure joy, my brothers and sisters, whenever you face trials of many kinds, because you know that the testing of your faith produces perseverance. Let perseverance finish its work so that you may be mature and complete, not lacking anything.
JAMES 1:2–4

Note from the Author

I absolutely love writing dual-timeline stories. This book has been so much fun to write—even if it was a little weird to be writing about a Steven and Kayla that weren't actually my kids. But I'm so glad I chose to name them after my daughter and son-in-love. If you've read any of my books, you know I love suspense. Every story has at least a little snippet of it, and in this one, I got to use my all-out love for it. I hope you have enjoyed *Bridge of Gold.*

While I have done extensive research on so many different things for this project, I did have to take some artistic license in certain areas. Any mistakes are obviously my own, but please know that my heart for accuracy, including historical accuracy, is true. At times, though, it's not possible to know the exact truth of circumstances or how things were done.

I had to learn a lot about diving—past and present—and spoke with several experts in the area. I will go to great lengths to research things for my readers, but I drew the line at actually diving myself. Especially when I knew what I wanted to do to my characters. Let's just say, I really enjoy breathing. Above the water.

If you are as fascinated with how the Golden Gate Bridge was built as I am, here are some links that might interest you.

https://www.goldengate.org/exhibits/working-under-water/
https://www.goldengate.org/assets/1/6/ggb-exhibit3-1_3-4.jpg

https://www.goldengate.org/assets/1/6/ggb-exhibit3-1_4-3.jpg
https://www.goldengate.org/assets/1/6/ggb-exhibit3-1_3-1.jpg

The Doors to the Past Series is so exciting, as it highlights great national and historic monuments. Make sure you check out the rest in the series. *The Lady in Residence* by Allison Pittman and *Hope between the Pages* by Pepper Basham are both available now, with more to come!

Enjoy the journey, and thank you for reading.

Kimberley Woodhouse

Kimberley Woodhouse is an award-winning and bestselling author of more than twenty-five fiction and nonfiction books. A popular speaker and teacher, she's shared her theme of "Joy through Trials" with more than two million people across the country at more than two thousand events. Kim and her husband of twenty-nine-plus years have two adult children. She's passionate about music and Bible study and loves the gift of story.

You can connect with Kimberley at www.kimberleywoodhouse.com and www.facebook.com/KimberleyWoodhouseAuthor

More from Doors to the Past Series...

Hope Between the Pages
by Pepper Basham

Clara Blackwell helps her mother manage a struggling one-hundred-year old family bookshop in Asheville, North Carolina, but the discovery of a forgotten letter opens a mystery of a long-lost romance and undiscovered inheritance which could save its future. Forced to step outside of her predictable world, Clara embarks on an adventure with only the name Oliver as a hint of the man's identity in her great-great-grandmother's letter. From the nearby grand estate of the Vanderbilts, to a hamlet in Derbyshire, England, Clara seeks to uncover truth about family and love that may lead to her own unexpected romance.

Paperback / 978-1-64352-826-7 / $12.99

Undercurrent of Secrets (Coming September 2021)
by Rachel Scott McDaniel

As wedding coordinator for the 100-year-old steamboat the Belle of Louisville, Devyn Asbury takes pride in seeing others' dreams come true, even though her engagement had sunk like a diamond ring to the bottom of the Ohio River. When the Belle becomes a finalist in the Timeless Wedding Venue contest, Devyn endeavors to secure the prestigious title with hopes to reclaim some of her professional dreams. What she hadn't planned on was Chase Jones showing up with a mysterious photo from the 1920s.

A century earlier, Hattie Louis is as untamable as the rivers that raised her. As the adopted daughter of a steamboat captain, her duties range from the entertainment to cook. When strange incidents occur aboard the boat, Hattie's determined to discover the truth. Even if that means getting under First Mate Jack Marshall's handsome skin.

Paperback / 978-1-64352-994-3 / $12.99